TELL ME A STORY

Appalachian Tales

Elizabeth Hardin Buttke

Jan-Carol Publishing, Inc

"every story needs a book"

Tell Me a Story
Elizabeth Hardin Buttke

Published June 2019
Little Creek Books
Imprint of Jan-Carol Publishing, Inc
All rights reserved
Copyright © 2019 by Elizabeth Hardin Buttke
Front Cover Painting: Elizabeth Hardin Buttke
Graphic Design: Tara Sizemore

ISBN: 978-1-950895-05-2
Library of Congress Control Number: 2019943620

You may contact the publisher:
Jan-Carol Publishing, Inc
PO Box 701
Johnson City, TN 37605
publisher@jancarolpublishing.com
jancarolpublishing.com

To all of those that love a good story. Enjoy.

Acknowledgments

Thank you to all my readers who have loved and supported my writing. Also, thank you to my family. Without them, there wouldn't have been so many great memories. Special thanks to artist Helen Cook Lowe for helping me believe that anything you accomplish is deserving of praise.

Melodies of Home

To my ears comes the sound of water as it moves over the creek bed of rocks, pebbles, and sand. Up the bank rests the roots, all twisted and brown, that give life to the large tree growing almost out of the water. Branches that hang like many knurled fingers reach out over the pasture's edge. Green, lumpy grass spreads into a wide view in front of me. A lone apple tree sits in the corner of the field, yielding a tasty treat for the cattle and occasional deer.

My heart and mind are flooded with memories of long ago and move through me like the wind dancing over the pasture grass. I see a field, my mamaw's house, and the pictures in my head come to life.

There's my uncle, leading Fred, the big, red workhorse, from the barn to the edge of the field. He stops to make sure his plow is in place. With harness straps draped across his shoulders, he places his hands on the plow handles. Giving a click with his cheek and tongue, head down, the horse starts his first row. Dust and dirt roll up from the blades and hooves.

Sitting close by under a tree in the yard is my mamaw in her bonnet, along with my mom and aunt, all in their work clothes of skirts and cotton blouses. The hoes have been sharpened beforehand, and they wait to tidy the newly planted tobacco plants and smooth the dirt around the roots. My cousins and I are left to wonder and play, climbing on the gigantic rock beside my mamaw's house, running up the hill to the grape-vine, rolling down the hill over the soft, warm grass. Feet are bare, and tiny, young legs can be seen as if growing from under the girls' dress tails. All the boys race and play in the dirt in their worn, denim pants of different colors, knees patched for double endurance.

We were all family...living in a wide half-circle around mamaw's house. Paths led from her back door to each house like veins leading from a heart. Every path was well worn, beaten down from years of being traveled, looking like small dirt roads. A big plum tree stood at the corner of the can-house, heavy with soon-to- ripen fruit. Inside the cool walls and the earthen floor of the can-house were the garden, tobacco sprays, and fertilizer. Spools of twine, shovels, and hoes were propped in every corner. Bins on both sides stored the potatoes, onions, apples, and turnips, along with this and that. The pungent smell of ammonia, mixed with the notable musty odor of aged dirt, met you as the wooden door was opened.

The day was alive. A cool breeze was blowing, bees were buzzing, and butterflies hungrily drank from the endless choice of flowers that decorated the yard. Looking over the field, the trio had started hoeing, the horse and plow always a few rows ahead. Reflections from the sun brightly glinted off the tin that covered the spring-house sitting in the middle of the tobacco patch. When the sun was high and stomachs were growling, everyone would take a break. My uncle would bring the horse to the chestnut tree and unburden him of the plow. With the harnesses secured to the tree, he was left in the shade to munch on the grass, with a bucket of cool water close by, while the adults snacked on a pack of peanut butter crackers or a Little Debbie cake. The kids drank a cup of Kool Aid, usually with a peanut butter and jelly sandwich. Leaned up against a tree, my mom, my aunt, and my mamaw would relax and fan their faces, laughing and talking. Then, back to the field they went till the job was done. Soon, the rows of plants were chopped clean of any weeds, dirt smoothed and tucked around each one like a blanket. They called it 'a day.'

Fred stood solemnly, his slick, red hide quivering to keep the buzzing flies away. The old workhorse and farmer were tired, but in a satisfying way. There would be fruits from their labor, and that made it all worthwhile. Us youngun's stood by, eagerly waiting to see who would get to ride way up high on Fred's broad back as he ambled his way back to the barn. Usually, my uncle would lift three of us up, and then we held on to each other, feeling as big and brave as an Indian Chief, enjoying the ride and tingling with excitement.

It wasn't necessarily the *things* that made life seem so easy and carefree...it was a feeling, to be young and feel loved, to feel safe, and to not have a care in the world.

I think back through memories of lying in the bed at night after mom had made sure our feet were clean and our faces were washed and most importantly, the family kneeling in the living room while mom and dad prayed. Then, sweet sleep would soon settle the house. The opened windows would beckon the night air, the lullaby of the crickets, the 'ribbits' of the frogs, and the occasional hoot of an owl. The creek would softly play the melody they all sang to.

Closing my eyes, I sigh...and smile. We were living the best years of our lives and didn't even realize it. A light breeze blows across my face, and I can see, smell, and touch those days of long ago. The emotions and longing for my days of youth build up and overflow my heart. Is that rain? Opening my eyes, I reach up and touch my cheek, and a tear meets my fingertips. Closing my eyes, I drift back.

Dirt roads and wooden bridges that groaned and creaked when a car or truck passed over them. Swimming holes, playhouses, barn swings made of twine. Camping out with just a quilt and a pillow on the dewy ground. Pretending to be anything I wanted to while the stars and moon lit up the night in a soft, white light. Telling all the ghost stories I had ever heard. Laughing as chills ran up my arms and legs. Everybody's dad was their hero, and our moms could fix anything. Bee stings, scratches, cuts, and even bumps on the head...moms could make it all better. All it took was the sound of her voice or the touch of her hand.

Pondering through my thoughts, I can still hear the screen door slam as each one came and went. Stepping out onto a porch made of wide, sawmill boards, weathered and gray, nails squeaked and groaned while being crossed over as some steps were rushed, or heavy, the sound echoing behind us. Birds are singing. A line of freshly washed sheets, shirts, and dresses snap and dance as the wind picks up, then lays low again. Sounds that one day we will long to hear. Like momma calling us to supper or waking us in the morning. The melody of life...sweet melody of love.

But let us not forget the smells. A dear friend to sights and sounds. It's there when you step into the kitchen of a mom, grandmother, or aunt. There they stand at the stove, one hand on a hip, the other stirring. Something is sizzling in the cast-iron skillet, and the oven is still warm from the pan of bread sitting on the table, steam ghost-like, drifting above it. On the days she's canning, the heavy, spicy smell of vinegar and spices sting your nose. Maybe it's chow-chow, or pickles, but whatever it may be, it leaves the house with a fragrance that can't be bottled and seeps into every corner of the house. Canning jars line the table to be filled with the colorful fruits and vegetables.

There's a saying that everything has its own scent, and oh, is it true. Like the blouse of a mom when you bury your head down to have a cry or give a tight hug. The splash of after-shave on a Sunday morning as Dad gets ready for church. It drifts through the back door, and before you even see them, you know who it is just by the smell. Mix that with a hug or a toss into the air by an uncle or dad, the laughter ringing through the house. One day, you will close your eyes and try to remember, and as if by magic, you can catch the scents on a breeze. Old-Spice...I will never forget the smell of Old-Spice.

Do I feel happy, or am I sad? No...I'm homesick for all of it. The feeling is sweet and lonesome, an ache you love but also hate. The past is set in stone, just like a grave marker, and you can never relive it. Remember the song "Precious Memories?" Well...that's what they are now. Feelings, way down deep inside us, and they stand proudly beside all the other emotions.

It's the excitement of the night before Christmas. The tree we cut from the mountain stands as beautiful as one from today's tree farm, decorated in the big, glowing, colorful electric bulbs. Silvery strands of 'Icicles' drape almost every pine needle. Little ornaments made from school were placed so everyone could see them, and we felt proud our mom still loved to hang them. Then, lying in bed, it seemed I could hear every tick of the clocks in the house as I waited for morning. Excitement took over my body like a plague, but sleep always won.

I remember, we would get in such a state of anticipation waiting for our dad to get home from work. Noses pressed against the window. Soon, his car would pull into the driveway. Jumping off the couch, we waited at the door. In he would come, big smile on his face. Then, he would swing each of us by our arms for a minute or two, back and forth between his legs. Sitting his lunch box on the table, we opened the black, metal lid, and like little birds, our small hands would dig around to find something good he didn't finish. Joy...the innocent kind.

We had genuine feelings for everything, from our elders to our parents, the little dog lying in the yard, or the poor, beautiful butterfly beside the road, no longer flying. These milestones of sadness and respect prepared us for their use later on in life.

We used to fear 'the look,' but a smile and a gentle hand motioning us over made us all warm inside. No one's real name was hardly ever called. It was usually honey, sugar, you handsome, or pretty little thang. Deep down inside, without us knowing it, the little seed of kindness was planted with this nurturance. Life's music notes float right along like a feather on a breeze, till one day, the song gets a little sadder. People we love start leaving us, as if we are pulling petals from a flower. The more we pull, the less pretty it is. We search for things to fill their places, finding nothing, but they have left us reminders everywhere in our hearts.

So, now we sit, trying to clear the clutter built up from over the years in our minds, hoping to feel for just a second, or maybe a minute, those fading memories. Like a puzzle with all the pieces once you put it together, the picture is beautiful.

Here, there are no hundreds of miles between us and loved ones. There are no tombstones with names and dates. It's a moment of peace, a dream while we are awake, and we hold on with all our might.

Sisterly Love

Oh my goodness...I can only imagine what it was like growing up with these two girls, the middle two of four sisters, with six brothers above and below them in age. Life must have been a challenge to get attention, alone time, or even to just have something that was all theirs, not having to share it with anybody. They were close in age; maybe this is why they ended up with a close bond to each other. They played together, got into trouble together, and later, they even went on dates together. Yes, they were close. Whispering late at night under the covers and giggling about all the silly little things in the way all girls do, their mom would holler up the stairs for them to hush and go to sleep before they woke their little sister up. The oldest sister had left home at a young age, mostly going from state to state, living out her zest for life and fancy things.

She would come in from time to time. Opening her suitcase, she would let them dress up in her fluffy petticoats and high heels and paint their lips red with lipstick that rolled up through the shiny, silver tube. Oh, they envied their older sister. It seemed like she had everything, but she would almost snatch their hair out if they broke a heel off a shoe or ripped a petticoat, and then they wished she would leave again. The oldest brother had married and left home by then too, and he would stop in occasionally. After he slid out of his truck, they would run down the yard to meet him. He gave each one a piece of candy, but for the two sisters, he would reach in the other pocket, pull out a plug of tobacco, and cut both of them a little piece with his pocket knife. Smiling, they would wrap their arms around his waist, giving a big hug, and then run off to chew the tobacco. Most days were spent like this, happy and fun, but not all days were.

It was a kind of lazy, summer day, when one of the sisters came through the yard chewing on a piece of gum.

"Let me chew it for a while, Margaret!" Loretta begged.

"No, you should have saved yours." Margaret replied, getting irritated at her pleading.

"I'm going to tell Mommy if you don't!" Loretta threatened.

"Go ahead; I don't care." Margaret answered smugly.

Well, it wasn't long till their mom came out the back door, slamming the screen door as it shut. She had things better to do than hear them fight over a piece of chewing gum.

"Margaret!" she hollered. "Come here right now," she demanded.

Creeping around the side of the house, she came, mad, but meek, and stood before her mom.

"Now, you let her chew it for a while, or I'll throw it in the trash. You hear me?" Looking at Margaret, she shook her finger at her as she talked.

"Okay, I will. Just let me have five more minutes," Margaret pleaded as Loretta stood to the side smirking at her.

"Five more minutes, and I better not have to come back out here," their mom warned them. Turning, she went back inside.

"You go around and wait on the front porch. I'll bring it to you in a minute," Margaret sweetly told her sister.

Arms crossed, Loretta went around the house to wait. Having won the fight, she was feeling quite happy. Margaret, on the other hand, was as mad as a wet hen, and she wasn't about to lose that easily. Her younger brothers played up by the grapevine. Walking around, she acted like she was just killing a little time as she watched the ground. It didn't take long till she found what she was looking for. Laying in a small clump of grass was a small splat of chicken poop. She almost laughed out loud. Sitting down, she slyly took the gum out of her mouth, pulled it open some, then scooped up the poop and wrapped it nicely in the gum. Jumping up, she ran to let her big-mouth sister have her turn. There she sat, legs crossed, one foot swinging in triumph. Slowly climbing the steps, Margaret held out the gum.

"Here you go, big baby," she smiled as she handed the gum to Loretta.

"Thank you," Loretta replied, plummy. Throwing the gum in her mouth, she raced off the porch to enjoy her victory. That didn't last long. Margaret didn't even have time to sit down before hearing the results of her trick. Around the side of the house, the sounds of gagging, puking, and crying could be heard like a dinner bell ringing. Hiding behind the bush at the corner of the porch, Margaret watched. There, Loretta was doubled over at the chimney, her breakfast now lying on the ground, tears and spit streaming off her face. Before long, it seemed like the whole family was gathered around her. Margaret panicked as she saw her mom wiping her sister's face with her apron, then opening her mouth and poking a finger in to try and rid her of whatever was making her sick. Someone shoved a glass of water in Loretta's hand and told her to swish it around and spit. Margaret didn't move. Her heart was pounding, and her legs were shaky. It seemed like an eternity before Loretta could talk and tell their mom what Margaret had done. One of the bigger boys picked her up, carrying his sick sister into the house. Hands on her hips, their mom looked around the yard, eyes scanning every corner and bush, looking for the guilty culprit. It wasn't long till she saw the one bush that was shaking. Margaret watched as she walked angrily, never taking her eyes off the bush. Reaching in, she pulled Margaret out.

Well, you can imagine the rest. Margaret got the best little switching ever. After that, both girls cried, but her sister never asked to share her gum again.

It wasn't long till they had forgiven each other, and their days went back to normal. For how long, you ask? Well, for as long as it took for another opportunity to present itself, which happened to be some months later. Loretta had somehow gotten a boil right on her stomach, right below her belly button. By that point, it was huge, red, and painful. All she could do was sit with the waist of her knee length shorts pulled down, leaned back, trying not to move. Taking her little sister with her, Margaret decided to walk up to the 'sweet' apple tree in the pasture and get some to eat on. Munching on one and holding the other two, she came back to the front porch to sit and enjoy them. There sat Loretta, poultice rag laying on her stomach, in misery.

"Can I have one, Margaret?" she asked in a painful voice.

"No, if you want one, go get it yourself!" Margaret replied matter-of-factly to her.

Loretta moaned and groaned, wanting one of the apples, and Margaret got madder and madder from listening to her. She finally got tired of hearing her and stood up on the bottom step.

"There!" she practically screamed. Raring back with one in her hand, she threw it at Loretta. A wild panther couldn't have screamed any louder than Loretta did as the hard, little green apple hit the boil on her stomach dead center. Margaret's hands flew to her mouth as she watched her sister double over, realizing she hadn't caught the apple. Rushing to her, she repeated over and over that she was sorry. Then, there came their mom, once again, to see what in the world had happened now. Margaret had started crying and was trying to explain that she hadn't meant to hurt Loretta. Gently, their dear mom pulled the poultice away from Loretta's stomach. The impact from the apple had busted the boil, relieving the sore of all the infection and getting it all over Loretta. If she could have gotten up, I don't think there would be a Margaret here today. Words went around like a windmill between the three. Finally, their mother had it all cleaned up and was looking it over. Needless to say, the horrible incident actually turned out to be just the thing that needed to be done. After that, the boil was gone, and aside from being sore for a while, Loretta could get up and move without pain. She didn't let Margaret off that easily though. For days, she held a grudge. Then, one day, a truce was called after Margaret gave Loretta a piece of tobacco to chew on that she had been saving. Once again, they were best friends.

Years to come, they would look back and laugh at these milestones of life, wondering how their mom survived them and eight more.

November Tears

He sat there in the old truck, motor running and a steady, white cloud coming from the tail pipe. How long, he didn't know; it was dark now. Tears ran down the many wrinkles on his face as he gently ran his weathered hand along the dash, talking to the truck like an old friend. The windows had fogged up some from the cold and rain outside. Fall was slowly fading to winter. Looking towards the church, he could barely see the soft glow of the lamp through the stained glass window that now kept his loving wife of almost sixty years company as she lay in a coffin of cedar.

"Yes." His voice quivered now as he spoke to himself. "You both have given me a happy and meaningful life. We've been down some rough roads, but we had some beautiful rides together. Both of you have been strong, even when you carried a heavy load." He leaned in closer to the windshield. His heart melted looking at the beautiful glow of red coming from the church window. He hated to leave her.

"Come on ole girl," he whispered to the truck. "Let's leave and let her rest."

As if feeling his sadness, the motor quietly shifted into gear, and the truck took an old friend around the church one last time. Passing the cemetery, they could see the mound of dirt waiting in the shadows of the trees and moon light. The cold ground and leaves made a crackling sound as the tires rolled down the split-rail fence line.

He was a lonesome figure going down the road in the white glow of the moon, back bowed from the years of hard work. The traditional, trucker style hat now sat a little looser on his balding head, aged and worn from the countless times of taking it off to wipe his brow before placing it back on again. Work boots that laced above his ankles were a little heavier on his tired and bony feet. His legs quivered as he pressed the clutch and gas pedal. Chugging down the road, truck springs a'groaning, his eyes kept a steady gaze on the familiar road ahead of him.

Rounding the last bend, he could see the shadowy shape of the barn, then the golden, yellowish glow coming from the window of the house. He parked the truck beside the house, as usual. 'Maybe I'll just sleep out here tonight,' he thought, but the curling smoke from the house chimney beckoned him to come in and warm his aching joints.

Shutting the truck door, he turned and prepared himself to face the fact she wouldn't be sitting in her chair when he opened the door. The old barn cat came across the porch, meowing as she circled around his legs.

"Come on ole girl," he said, chuckling as he opened the door. "Guess it's just you and me now."

The warmth from the wood stove welcomed them both. Shuffling to the kitchen, he thought of making coffee but wandered to the sink to look out the window that overlooked the yard. Squinting, his eyes focused on the clothesline over by the lilac bush. The cat jumped on the counter to peer out with him.

"Do you see that, Snowball?" he whispered with curiosity. Standing at the post was a willowy, white form of a woman. His heart beat faster as his eyes beheld the form. Then, like a dandelion blown in the wind, she was gone.

"Oh my goodness, Snowball!" he exclaimed, his voice now brittle, but happy. "She ain't gone; she's just waiting on me now." Gently, he soaked the tears up with the white fur of the old cat. Making his way back to the wood stove, he settled himself in the rocking chair, cat curled up in his lap.

He didn't get to see his wife's beautiful funeral or hear all the good things the preacher told of her. He wasn't there when they placed her in the ground and covered her grave, placing the wreaths of flowers all around. No...the next morning, John Bridges found him dead, still sitting peacefully in the rocking chair, the cat asleep in his lap. The only thing he got to do was take the last ride with her, only it wasn't in a truck this time.

Inlaws and Outlaws

In every state, town, and county, there's that one community with the 'brand' of a mean place. Living in a small mountain community as I did, we all knew where the bad one around there was. We had heard the stories. Every once in a while, my mom would get me, and we would ride there to see her best friend. This place was located right across the state line, just a few miles above our house. I remember feeling like I was traveling hundreds of miles away from home into the badlands, expecting that any minute, a bad guy would jump out and just shoot us or beat us up like the stories I had heard. Nothing ever happened of course, but the trip would bring back memories for my mom, and she would tell me another 'hair- raiser.'

Every man there carried a gun. The law was so far away, nobody bothered to call them if something happened. They just took care of it themselves, and nothing was said. One brother had shot the other over a guitar. Another man had shot and killed seven and never spent a night in jail over any of it! Some man got his stomach sliced open, and his guts fell out. They just laid him on the kitchen table, washed his guts off in a dish-pan, put them back in, and sewed him up. Nope...this wasn't a place to take a Sunday drive to unless you were with somebody that lived there or you were going to visit someone you knew there. They didn't take to strangers and didn't trust anybody but close family. Even then, if you did somebody wrong, sooner or later, you'd get what was coming to you.

Later on, when I was old enough to start liking boys, my mom started telling me the sweet side of this place. They may have been mean over there, but, gosh, were there some good looking boys there too! Then, she had my attention...a little something worth the risk. My mom and her sister had dated lots of boys from there back in the day. She'd talk about how nice and charming some were...tall, dark, and handsome... how they could sing and play any instrument—all that good stuff. She came close to sticking with a few from over there herself, but that wasn't her destiny. No...she was spared, but me...I got a good dose of all that when I was barely sixteen.

He saw me get off the school bus one day as he and a friend were going back across the mountain. The wheels of how he was going get to me started turning in his head. About a year or so later, we were married, and momma wasn't lying. He was tall, dark, and had the bluest eyes you had ever seen. He also carried the last name of one of the most feared families over there. My mom had even dated his dad and uncles when she was young. Because I was her daughter, they were all pretty good to me and watched out for me.

After moving over there, I began to see a little of the bad side I had always heard of. Every man did carry a gun.

Grudges were still held between families. You didn't want to be around if someone pulled out a jar of Moon-Shine, that's for sure.

My first lesson came one night at a birthday party for a cousin of my husband. Some were outside standing around a bonfire. The rest, including me, were in the house, sitting around and talking. Then, somebody started passing the jar. When it got to me, I declined and passed it on. I never was a drinker. After a few passes, people were laughing and having a good time, when the thunderous sound of a chain-saw shook the walls from the kitchen. Next thing you know, you can't hear anything but the roar of the chain-saw. Everybody jumped up to go look. I was scared to death. I had never been around any kind of craziness. Then, there he came, the cousin's husband, fueled with fire-water and jealously, both hands on the saw. Holding our ears, we dodged and scooted around to get out while he sawed the table in two, then started on the legs of every piece of furniture standing. Making it outside, the picnic table and things were also sawed in two. We asked somebody what had happened. Evidently, he caught his wife and someone flirting around and decided to destroy their home like she had destroyed their love. We left...and fast. The next morning, the making up began, and everything was fine. They stayed together for years, opened a restaurant, and had a little girl.

Nevertheless, I learned that alcohol and a bunch of people gathered together hardly ever ends well.

One place where my husband and I lived was down a little dirt road. A man owned two little houses that were separated by a small field. We lived in the second one. We were friends with the couple above us, so we would visit each other and hang out some. Lying in bed one night, we heard a gun being fired. We both crawled over to the window that faced their house. Bullets were hitting the house, making a smacking sound; we got down in the floor just in case. We stayed put and waited till morning. Leaving, we drove slowly by the house. Nobody was around. Bullet holes were everywhere, and windows were shot out. Later, we found out someone had accused the guy of stealing off him and had come for revenge. That's just how serious these people were. We ended up moving in with my mother-in-law for the time being, which was not a good idea since I wasn't her pick for her son.

The house sat right off a little paved road that went across another mountain. On the other side was her garden, a small field, and a creek running down beside it. Then, you had her sister-in-law and husband that lived on the other side of the creek through another field. My husband's mom and dad had been divorced for years by now, but he would come by quite often. I don't remember what had started the disagreement between him and his sister's husband across the creek, but late one evening, he came in furious.

Picking up the phone, he called their house, asking to speak to her husband. First words out of his mouth were, "I'm coming to kill you; just be waiting!" Out the door he went as we all watched from the picture-window. Gun in hand, he crossed the road, walking in a rush towards the garden. It had gotten dark, so we couldn't really see anything but his shadow moving. About the time he reached the garden, a gun was fired. One shot. Of course, my husband and his sister ran out the door to find their dad because there was no other shot fired.

They found him in the garden, shot through the hip. He was soon taken to the hospital. I guess you don't call another man to tell him you're coming to kill him because he's going to be waiting for you.

He never really recovered enough to walk without crutches, and nobody was charged with anything.

Don't get me wrong, there was just as much fun as there was ducking. We had things like pig roasts and bonfires on dirt roads off in the woods, people just sitting around relaxing, telling big tales. The little country store was owned by the sweetest couple, and they sold a bologna sandwich that tasted better than any steak! We fished, rode motorcycles, and camped at the river, just a lot of nice outdoor things. Pretty soon, I had had about enough of the guns, fights, and stuff, so I packed up and moved back to good ole Tennessee. But if you ever want to visit and get a little taste of the wild west...just cross the state line.

Mother & Medicine

Growing up, most of us depended on our moms to make everything better...bumps, scrapes, cuts...everything right down to a broken heart. If you got sick, she didn't put you in the car and send you off to the doctor. No...she went to her special cabinet. The medicine cabinet.

Usually found in the bathroom or kitchen, sometimes behind the bathroom mirror or one of the many cabinet doors in the kitchen, the medicine cabinet was where you would find iodine, baby aspirin, castor oil, ointments of every sort, and rags from dad or your brother's old t-shirts for bandaging. There was no need for bandage tape; just rip, tear two strings at the end, and tie in a knot.

Germ killer or lamp oil, but hopefully not the rubbing alcohol, were usually used as peroxide. Once, I was up at the branch, swinging from a tree limb, and then I dropped to the ground and continued to play with my friends. Soon, every-body was noticing blood splats on the rocks and ground. We all stopped and began checking ourselves out. Sure enough, when I looked at the bottom of my foot, the heel was gashed open and bleeding. When I had dropped, a broken coke bottle had cut me. Terrified and crying, I hopped to the house. The first thing my dad did was sit me on the edge of the porch and pour the lamp oil to the cut. This was to keep things from getting sore and to help it heal. I still ended up having to get stitches for the first time. The doctor advised for me to come back to get them removed, but instead, mom just held me down, got her eyebrow tweezers, and took them out herself.

Sometimes, we were just doctored like everything else around the house. Take a dog for instance. None of our dogs ever had rabies shots, but they never missed a worming. They would hold their mouths open and put the medicine in or hide it in the food. One way or another, they got wormed religiously till they started filling out and had a healthy look. The same thing happened to us. By three, we were automatically wormed. People had a fear of worms crawling up in a youngun's throat and choking them. After that, if we started picking at our food or pulling at our bottoms, we had better start looking out because mom would run us down... and we would run because that stuff was awful. She tried to hide it in orange juice or apple sauce, but nothing could cover that taste. One way or another, we got wormed again for good measure. After that, we tried real hard not to look 'peaked.' Even when I had my own kids and grandkids, I made sure they got wormed once before the age of four. I would still advise it.

Most medicine back then tasted pretty good. The cough medicine wasn't bad. The children's laxative wasn't bad either... another thing that was given to us occasionally to "clean them younguns' stomachs out." But the best was the baby aspirin. They were little, pink, soft pills, and we thought they were yummy. My cousins and I would eat the whole bottle like candy if we found them. We got into trouble for it, but it was worth it to us.

I guess the one thing that made us all cry was the Merthiolate, or iodine. Every scratch or scrape had to have that stuff, and it would set us on fire...not to mention the fact that it resulted in us going around with our skin red like stripes. Before the hard, plastic stick that connected to the lid came out of the bottle, we were crying.

My mamaw used to pick up every baby by the heels and roll it across her lap to help with liver growth. I watched her do some. Babies were also given catnip for hives. You didn't want a baby hiving, according to their teachings. Of course, when one of mine was hiving and wasn't sleeping well, here came my mom with the catnip. I just prayed.

Yep...they had a cure for everything. Burdock root for boils and things. SS tonic to build your blood. Honey and liquor for coughs. The list goes on and on. The one thing I still laugh about to this day is the time when I had a sore on my face. I went in mamaw's back door, and right behind it, she had a pie-safe that held some of her remedies. "Sissy," she said, "that sore ain't getting any better, so come here." After rummaging around, she reached for the white jar of cream with the blue label that had a cow on it. In my head, I knew it was for the cows, but you didn't dispute your mamaw. So, I stood there, holding my breath while she took a swipe with her finger and rubbed it on my sore, once again praying I didn't die. I lived, and the sore got better.

I realize now that she knew more than I did. When she was just six, she had cooked and helped raise two sisters after their mom died from child birth, standing on a wooden crate and cooking on a cook-stove while their dad worked. She was the oldest. People would say to their father, "Nat, ain't you afraid to leave them younguns home by themselves?" He would answer, "Why, I didn't leave them by themselves. I left the lord with them." Yes, my mamaw was a strong woman, in body and faith. She raised her children the same.

I think most all of us can agree that the best medicine out of any type of medicine cabinet was our momma's Bible.

The Rock Creek Boys

Oh, what can I say? They were a fun bunch for sure. The worst situations could be taken and turned into an all-out, he-ha time. I'm going to tell a few short stories about them. These boys left behind quite a few. Although most incidents were while they were drinking, all of them had a humble, kind side and grew up to be good men. Now, the Hardin boys always had fun. From a young age, they loved to play tricks and then stand back and laugh. Here are some examples:

Their mother had a houseful. At that time, there were four boys and maybe three girls at home. One of the oldest would get up early in the morning, supposedly to get the fire started in the cook-stove for his dear, sweet mother. After getting the fire going, he couldn't resist sprinkling black pepper on top of the stove. When the stove got hot, this would cause a sneezing fit for whoever got around it. Oh, but did he get a laugh out of watching everybody run to the stove to get warm, then sneeze their heads off. Their mom would sneeze and sniffle the whole time she was trying to cook their breakfast. But besides him, who knew?

These brothers also had one sister that was a little on the heavy side. When she was old enough to court a boy, she was all excited one day that he was coming to visit. Two of the brothers knew that when Bo came walking up, she would come bounding out of the house. They didn't have to think long; these ideas came as natural as breathing. So, taking a rope, they tied it tightly to each porch post coming down the steps. Then, they hid to watch. Sure enough, there the fine lad came. She saw him from the window. Throwing open the screen door, she came thundering across the porch to meet him. The rope caught her right above her ankles, causing her to tumble right out into the yard at his feet. Her brothers ran around laughing.

Now, the youngest child was a boy and was considered the mother's pet. Having had Asthma and breathing problems, he tended to be babied by her more. While doing the wash out in the yard on a scrub board one day, she asked the oldest boys to watch him. By then, they were in their early teens, and the youngest was about nine or ten. A while later, as she was hanging the clothes on the line, there came her baby boy through the yard, stumbling and falling around. The kind brothers watched from the creek as their mom checked him all over. It didn't take long before the smell caught her nose. They had watched him alright. Down at the creek, they had gotten him good and drunk on some liquor they had. She was fit to be tied, but the boys just laid down, rolling and laughing. It was worth every smack of the hand she gave to them.

The sisters, being a little jealous themselves, tried to give him a whipping every chance and reason they got. But being a Hardin, the youngest brother had caught onto a few tricks himself. When they chased him with the switch, he would run in the bedroom and jump on the bed, waiting for them. As soon as one of the sisters was close enough, he would throw a blanket over her head, jump off the bed, and run. I would say there was never a dull moment in that house. A good laugh was their best quality.

All the boys later joined the military. Most went into the Navy. The youngest joined the Marines. When he told her, his mother said she could have dug her grave with a spoon. Later, the boys were back, and Rock Creek was their stomping ground. The youngest Hardin boy had a jolly group of good-old-fellas to hang with. They would mostly run the roads in old jalopies and hang out at the park or an old cave they had found years ago, drinking and having fun. It was on one of these days, as they laid around a swimming hole and drank, that one of the gang jumped up, ripped off his t-shirt, and said, "Take me to town, boys. I want some new ones."

Piling into the car, they all went off to town. The fella went in the store and came out with a new pack of t-shirts. Holding them in his lap, he waited till they got back to the swimming hole. Getting out, they all went back to talking and drinking as he tore open the new t-shirts. Jerking one out to put on, he realized something was wrong. While he held it up, trying to see through his blurry vision, the other boys started laughing. In his state of mind, when he had bought the t-shirts, he hadn't bothered to look at the size and had gotten baby t-shirts. I guess those went into the fire.

Now, every man or boy believes in taking care of a good friend. You back them up, hold them up, and do whatever they might need. It wasn't long till an opportunity came knocking. One of their buddies had gotten sick and was in the hospital. Being a heavy drinker, he was going through some withdrawals, so the youngest Hardin and some pals offered to go sit with him and watch him. Of course, they snuck in a jar to sip on for the long night ahead. It must have been some good stuff because before long, they all passed out. While in their intoxicated sleep, their ailing pal fell out of his bed, adding a few knots and bruises on his head and body. The nurse was so mad, she told his buddies that were supposed to be watching him that they weren't fit to sit up with the dead and ran them off.

Most of us have had those times when we had good intentions of sticking with a friend no matter what, but then we saw that it could get us in a heap of trouble. Then, we weren't so sure. Once again, the youngest Hardin was up on Rock Creek, drinking with the boys, when one of them wanted to leave. Since the boy was too drunk to drive, Hardin decided to lay him in the back seat where he could sleep. Yep, like a good friend, he planned to drive him home and then come back afterward. He didn't get far down the road before he saw blue lights coming up behind him. Nope, Hardin wasn't going to jail for anybody. So, he turned the car lights off, got his speed just right, opened the car door, and jumped out, rolling out of sight. The dark car and backseat passenger went rolling on down the road. Where they stopped, I really don't know, but I'm sure good intentions were in Hardin's heart, and I'm sure the car and passenger both landed somewhere.

While they were lying in an old cave one night, drinking and goofing off, the boys got a little bored, I guess, and decided to completely blacken the face of one of their friends. Unknowingly, he stumbled home in the wee morning hours and knocked on the door for his mom to let him in. Looking out the window, she didn't recognize this fella at all and refused to open the door. Left out in the cold, he slept it off in the barn. Later, he realized what his dear friends had done. Even he had to laugh at the thought of his mom's reaction.

One of the fellas got married. He wasn't what you would call a good provider, and soon, the wife had had enough. The lights had been turned off due to him not paying the bill, so the judge gave him so many hours to have the lights back on for her and the children. "Yes sir," he promised, and he did. He went and lit a candle and sat it on the kitchen table. You had to be very specific with those Rock Creek boys.

As the years passed, each brother married and settled down, and the youngest Hardin later became my dad. There were some mornings when we woke up with mustaches made from stove soot. Mom would fix a cold glass of water and leave the room, and Dad would laugh and challenge us to see how fast we could drink a glass of water. Of course, we chugged it to win. Mom would come back, sit down, and reach out, bringing back an empty glass. It made her so mad. Sometimes, he would grease the car door handles with that thick, black grease, then laugh when we grabbed one and got a hand full. When I was younger, my dad had one of my friends convinced that he was so tough that he could eat glass. Of course, Dad said it in a way that the boy would never try it, just believe it. This little boy walked around like Hercules after Dad gave him a few motivational speeches.

Nowadays, he and I hunt for the best 'funnies' out of the paper or magazines. We still like to trick my mom and my brothers, laughing when we get a good one on them.

It's one trait I'm glad I inherited. Being an only girl with two brothers, tricks came in handy.

After marrying my mom, Dad quit drinking and running around with the boys, and well...to me, there is no better man.

Haints and Ghost

Some people believe in ghosts, and some people don't. However you believe, I don't think there are any of us who would turn down a good ghost story. There's just something about hearing these strange happenings that makes our scalps tingle and goose bumps crawl up our arms and legs. We love the stories. I personally like to leave that stuff alone. I like to hear the stories, but I don't meddle or hunt any ghosts.

I don't have to go far if I want to see a haunted house. My mamaw's house holds a lot of stories and strange sightings. Even *I* ran out of her house one day after an incident. She always said the dead wouldn't hurt you; it was the living you had to worry about. I will share a few of these stories with you, told to me by my mom, and moms don't lie. My mother grew up in this house. My papaw had torn down the old house there and built a new one in the same spot.

My mom and her sister were just young girls, and they had been on a double date with some boys from Shelton Laurel. When the boys brought them home, they all decided to sit in the car for a while before the girls had to go in. Suddenly, the one driving jumped in his seat, pointing out the window. All eyes in the car looked. Coming out from beside the kitchen chimney was a lady. She floated no higher than the tip of the grass blades. She was dressed all in white, as if wearing a wedding dress. Up the yard she floated, holding her gown off the ground with one hand. Soon, she disappeared into the trees. So real she was that the boys had gotten down in the floorboard of the car and covered their heads. As soon as the lady was gone, Mom and her sister fled the car and went into the house, and the boys left, gravel flying everywhere.

This same lady was seen again one night. My uncle and his wife had come in to visit and were sleeping in the bedroom beside my mamaw's. As they slept, his wife was awakened by a noise. Rising up on her elbows, she tried to scan the dark room to see where it was coming from. Slowly, the closet door opened, and there was the lady. Gracefully, she floated from the closet and left out of the bedroom door, leaving behind a terrified young couple.

After all my mamaw's kids had moved out, only she and the youngest son lived in the house. As I have told before, he was the baby and the family jewel. Almost thirty then, he considered himself to be a pretty tough guy, brave enough to chase down a bear, run through the woods all night, and hunt down some of the biggest game. To get upstairs, you had to come though his bedroom, and a door opened to the steps leading up.

Coming in late one night, he quietly undressed, got into bed, and snuggled down. Drifting off, he thought he had heard something. Sitting up in bed, he listened closely. Something was moving around upstairs. As quiet as a mouse, he reached beside his bed and laid the shotgun across his lap. After a moment, he could hear it better because slowly, it was walking down the stairs. 'Someone broke in through one of the upstairs windows,' he thought. Positioning himself, he raised the gun and waited for the person to open the door. Heart a'pounding, blood racing through his body, he was ready. Slowly, the door opened. From the glow of the street light, he watched. What came from behind that door was a man, but not a living one. He floated to the foot of my uncle's bed and looked at him. My uncle threw the gun in the floor, flew under the covers, and screamed for his mom. By the time she got to him, the ghost was gone. After telling her what happened, she just told him to lie down and go to sleep. "The dead wont hurt you." Easy for her to say...those things just didn't scare her. She said that at night, sometimes a ball of bright light would come into her bedroom and bounce from wall to wall, right next to the ceiling. She would just lie back down and go to sleep.

In 2010, my mamaw lay in her living room dying. It was her wish to die at home. The family was there, some in the house, some on the front porch, and some in the back yard. I had gotten home from work and walked over to check on her and sit with the family. Everyone was outside except for a couple of people sitting in the living room with her. We were all being quiet, just waiting. Getting up, I went through the living room door, past her bedroom, and into the bathroom. Sitting there, I was so sad, just thinking to myself, and then I heard my brother calling for our mom from the spare bedroom. 'Must be sitting in there to be alone,' I thought. "Mom!" he called. "Hey, mommy, come here." 'How rude,' I thought. 'He knows not to be hollering while our mamaw is sick and dying.' "Mom! Mom, come here." By then, I had pulled my pants up and was going to give him a mouth full. I came out of the bathroom in a huff and opened the bedroom door to let him have it. There was no one around but me. I could feel myself getting weak in the legs, and my skin crawled. Quick and quiet as a mouse, I got out of the house and then flew down the path to my mom's. I didn't even speak to anyone as I left, and my brother was at home. After telling Mom what had happened, she said it was probably my uncle, who they had all loved so dear, who had passed some years before, calling to his mother. Later that evening, my mamaw also passed.

I think the first house was haunted, and when my papaw built a new one in the same spot, those ghosts just moved in too.

The house stayed empty after she died. Heck, even when she was alive, we were scared to go to the bathroom, or even in the house, unless she was inside. No one even asked to live in it after she passed. The grandkids were too scared. It still sits. Alone.

A railroad track used to run across the top of my mamaw's land. All the way across the top of the mountain. It had been abandoned many years ago. We were told that on some nights, you could look up and see the lantern light as if the old man was checking the tracks. If it was a windy night, the light would sway and bounce in the dark night. Once or twice, we thought we saw it, but we weren't sure...or maybe we were just too scared to admit it because that was where we played. Nevertheless, there were other spooks in those mountains, so we had plenty to think on.

Winter Love

M s. Rose," the smiling, young nurse said, approaching Rose's chair. "Would you like some marshmallows in your hot cocoa?" Turning in her chair toward the voice, Rose's eyes glowed at the question as her mind, for a moment, took her back to another snowy day long ago.

The yearly vacation her family took was to a ski resort in North Carolina. After coming down with a cold, Rose was forced to spend most of the trip in the cozy, spacious lounge, curled up with a book in front of the enormous fireplace. She sat, sipping the hot cocoa and reading one of her many favorite books. One afternoon, she was reading and watching her family through the tall windows as they enjoyed the fluffy, white snow outside. From behind her, a soft, throaty voice asked, "May I enjoy the view with you for a while?" Turning on the soft, leather couch, she saw the most handsome boy her young eyes had ever seen. Blushing, she replied, "Please, have a seat. It does get lonely watching everyone having fun." Never taking his eyes off of her, he relaxed his tall, wiry frame into the chair next to her. "So, why aren't you out there in the snow?" she asked, smiling. "I think it's more beautiful in here," he answered, stretching his long legs across the pine flooring. "I haven't seen you out there either, ah..." "Rose. My name is Rose," she giggled "And I have a cold, so I am stuck inside." Leaning over, he looked into her mug. "Well, you know you will never get better unless you add marshmallows to that cocoa," he said, his face serious. "Really?" she asked suspiciously. Laughing, he stood. "Let me warm that up for you, Rose." Taking her mug, he walked to the counter. Coming back, he held two steaming cups of cocoa, marshmallows practically spilling over the rim. Gently, she took the mug into her hands.

For fifty-two years after that day, that would be how they celebrated every anniversary...there at the resort, sipping hot cocoa and marshmallows.

His young hands turned old and wrinkled with time. Soon, his heart gave out, and he had to leave his love behind. She buried him on a snowy, wintery day. To her, it couldn't have been more fitting.

"No, thank you, honey," she said now, answering the nurse. Rose couldn't stand the thought of someone else adding the sweetness to her cup, and no one ever did.

Big Brother, Big Trouble

Sissy was the middle child...right in the middle of two brothers. The youngest brother was sweet and kind of a serious type. Sissy was a small, timid girl and could be scared at the drop of a hat. But she had a vengeful side too, and she knew how to play her part in any situation like an Oscar winner. Roger, the older brother...well, like most older brothers, he liked to pester the younger two. It seemed Sissy got the biggest portion of this. This was just some of the loving aggravation her oldest brother put her through.

Roger knew she was afraid of everything, so having some fun out of her was always easy. Plus, she stuck her nose into everything he did. It was a warm summer day, and he and his friend from next door were out in the back yard playing 'camping out' with a sleeping bag. Sissy tagged along, begging the boys to let her sleep in it for a while. Finally, Roger got tired of this and decided to shut her up. "Okay, climb on in, and we'll zip you up," he told her. The sleeping bag was huge to her tiny, skinny frame. Lying still, she listened as the zipper started at her feet and then went up the side. But her brother didn't stop there. No, he zipped her all the way up, and then he and his friend walked off, leaving her in the back yard. Scared of the dark anyway, she fought and cried, trying to get out. There was no way. It's at times like these in kids' lives that I believe God watches out for such foolishness because just in time, their mom came out the back door and saw the commotion coming from the sleeping bag. Quickly, she unzipped it to find a sweaty, hysterical, little, redheaded girl who was scared to death. Roger got it from his mom when she found him.

He had to play with his sister some because sometimes there wasn't anybody else. So, one day, he decided to teach her to ride a bicycle. The big, red, worn-out bike was ready, and Roger held the handle bars so she could climb on. "Now, when I give you a push, you start peddling. Okay?" he instructed. Nodding her head, she held on tight, a little scared and a little excited. The back yard sloped down a hill and into a field. Giving her a big push, the bike took off rolling with the incline of the yard, a set of little feet trying to keep up. The further it went, the faster it got, and Roger was yelling, "Put your brakes on!" Sissy tried, but it was to no avail. She didn't stop till she crashed at the bottom, her body getting scratched up. Meeting her at the bottom, Roger grabbed the bike. "Give me the stupid thing. You can't ride." And off he went, leaving her crying, her knees still bleeding. It didn't help that later on their dad came home with a brand new tricycle for her younger brother. That wasn't fair at all to Sissy. Both boys had a bike, and she didn't. One day, she finally got her little brother to let her ride the shiny tricycle for a little while. When her mom called her in for the evening, the feeling of being left out on the bike deal slowly boiled inside her. Politely, she left the tricycle halfway under the back tire of her dad's car. Sure enough, when he left for work the next morning, he ran over it. It made her feel a little bad for her brother, but now she wasn't the only one without something to ride.

When she was six, the family moved back to her mom's home place. Her dad had given each of the children a lot for a house. Up there in the mountains, there were lots of things to do and plenty of friends to play with. But for some reason, little girls just can't leave big brothers alone, so Roger made her pay for all the time she spent tagging along and being nosey. Down at the creek in the back yard, there was a good swimming hole. Roger and his friends liked to have it all to themselves, so they made the smaller kids swim below it in the shallow water. To get this done, they convinced them the water was over their heads and that they would drown if they got in. Walking around on their knees, the water came to their chins, so the younger kids believed them. To the side, there was a huge rock, flat and long, that came down straight into the water. Sissy begged one day for her brother to just let her sit on that rock to watch them swim and jump off the rocks. Permission was given, so she climbed to the top of the rock to watch. By then, the rock was good and wet from all their splashing. Sissy sat, laughing and watching them. Roger climbed onto the rock on the opposite side to make his big jump. Hitting the swimming hole, the water splashed high and wide. Of course, Sissy got the most of it, which caused her to throw her hands up and move a little. Before she could even think, she slid like an ice cube straight into that dark, deep water. Once she hit the water, the fight was on with her trying not to drown and clawing for anything to save her. Laughing at her, Roger grabbed her. "Calm down!" he said, laughing as she fought for her life. Finally, he got her to listen for a second. "Stand up, you dummy." He laughed again. Standing, Sissy realized the water was really only waist deep on her. They had been tricking the younger kids all along just to have it to themselves. After that, everyone enjoyed the private pool.

Sissy wouldn't trust Roger to help her ride a bike, but maybe she could trust him to give her a ride. "Okay," he agreed one day when she asked. "You walk up to Aunt Loretta's driveway and wait on me. I ain't peddling there with you on the back. Too hard," he said. So, off she went, skipping up the driveway and then on up the road to wait. True to his word, there he came to get her. Sissy hopped on the seat, holding on tightly to his belt loops as he peddled standing up because the seat was small. They just had a small piece of road to travel before they would be at their driveway. When they were almost there, Roger turned his head, wind blowing his firey red hair all around, and hollered back at Sissy, "I forgot to tell you...I don't have any brakes!" "How do we stop?" she shrieked. "The creek!" he shouted, his voice bouncing with the bike. She screamed from the top of the driveway till the front tire hit the creek water, and then down they both went. Luckily, the yard there met the creek at a slight level. The water broke their crash some too. But once again, there she stood, soaked and crying. By then, their mom was tired of hearing Sissy, so her famous line became, "Well, you should've known better."

One Sunday, Sissy went to church with a friend, returning home before her mom and dad. By then, she was twelve, and Roger was fifteen. He hadn't gone to church that morning, so he was home. For some reason, they got into an argument, and they got mad fast. He ran her out of the house, cussing and hollering. Furious, she wasn't about to be out-done. She knew the one thing that no boy liked to be called, and that was an 's.o.b.' So, Sissy turned and yelled it in his face. Next thing she knew, he was coming out the front door with their mom's straw broom, jabbing her everywhere. She didn't have any shoes on, just her clothes and panty hose. Even though she was barefooted, he ran her up the driveway and on up the road, broom a'swinging every which way, church traffic coming down the road, and her running for her life. By the time she got away, her feet were burning from the gravel, and her panty hose were shredded. She didn't call him the bad word again either. Did she ever tear any of his things up for revenge...sure she did, and she told on him for everything, but she would also defend him like a wild cat if anyone else tried anything.

Siblings are like that, I guess. In the end, my brother Roger and I both survived each other. Our younger brother waited till about fourth grade before he caused any trouble. He hated school, and there wasn't anything he wouldn't do to get out of it. One school employee called him 'the meanest white boy God ever made.' He was expelled more than he went, and he was rarely allowed on the bus. That boy made up for all his quiet years. Brothers...you have to love them like a mother to get along with them.

Learning to Drive

I would have to say that my generation also had some pretty good hands-on moms. They didn't waste any time teaching us the first lessons in life, such as sitting up, talking, feeding ourselves, potty training, and most importantly, walking. These were the first necessities of life, and we learned them quickly. Our mothers were patient, but they were firm in their lessons.

I don't know about everybody else, but one of the most important lessons while growing up at my house was learning to drive. As soon as my siblings and I could sit on her lap and look over the steering wheel, Mom had us sitting there, hands on the wheel with hers, teaching us to drive...but not just in the yard or driveway. We started at the bottom of the mountain road leading home and drove all the way. When we mastered that, she would let go of the wheel and let us steer while she did the brakes and gas. Then came the last step...sitting in the driver's seat, Mom sitting close by, while we learned to steer and work the brake and gas peddles. We loved it, and I think she did too.

By the age of eleven, we could hop in the car and go anywhere if we were allowed. She didn't just want us to know how to drive; she wanted us to be able to get in any vehicle and go. "Sissy," she said one day. "I'm going to teach you to drive anything. That way, if you're out and need to get home, you can hop in and go." Soon, I could drive an automatic, a straight shift, and trucks with the gears on the column; if it had wheels, I could drive it. I learned to ride dirt bikes too. Later, I wasn't worried if I was out and wanted to go home when nobody else did. I just told them to throw me their keys, and I was gone. Someone told me one time that they were sorry because their car was a straight shift. I just smiled and told them, "My mom taught me to drive everything."

We didn't have new, smooth-driving cars. With some, we had to pump the gas just enough or wiggle the switch a little... all kinds of stuff. The only instruction I feared a little was the 'pump the brakes some or you won't stop.' I had good reason too. My dad had a car, and I was going to drive it up to my aunt's, which was just two driveways up from our house. "Don't forget to pump the breaks, Sissy," I was told before I took off. And I didn't...until I came back down the road and turned into our driveway. I put the brakes on, and to the floor they went. I got the car steered in-between the house and garage, but in the process, I forgot to pump the brakes. A big Poplar tree stopped me dead still, keeping me from going into the creek. Mom and Dad had heard me hit the tree and came running out the back door. There I sat, breath knocked out of me from the steering wheel and tears streaming down my face. I think I was twelve. There were both of them, one laughing and the other saying, "I told you to pump those brakes!" 'All's well that ends well' is all

I have to say about that. So far, thank God, that has been my only minor wreck.

The wrecker-service then was another car and a chain. Sometimes, the cars would break down beside the road, and somebody would either come along and pull you home or take you to get somebody to help you. At home, most times, I steered the broken car while someone pulled it. Mom never cared much for this. I liked it then, but I'm not sure about now. We do a lot of things growing up that we wouldn't do now. I haven't changed a tire since my twenties. But by watching my dad, if I had a flat tire back then, I knew exactly what to do. Trust me; we would eventually have a flat or blowout because the tires were always used when they were bought. Buying a tire, or tires, was like buying a new horse or cow for some. The man would roll it, bounce it, and run his hands over the rubber like petting a snake...gently. He'd check the tread to see if it was worn more on one side than the other, then turn it this way and that way before making the cheap purchase. And then when they went flat or blew out, he would swear they were dry-rotted to keep from looking not-too-sharp to others. It wasn't a problem though; just plug it and drive on.

The only thing I was never taught was to drive on snow. I still don't unless it's an emergency. I've had maybe four so far. The biggest one was when I was in Mars Hill, North Carolina. This was way before the big interstate was built. All you had were curves and mule-faced hills. Two lanes. A friend and I had visited some people, and right before dark, it started pouring the snow. They wanted us to spend the night, but my friend didn't want to drive back across the mountain. I wanted to go home. This being the last resort, I drove. Soon, there were two to three inches on those mountain roads. Going back, it was mostly uphill for a while, then downhill the rest of the way. The only thing I remembered my dad saying about snow was to get a steady speed and not to hit your brakes or let off. I clutched the steering wheel like a life raft and did just that, praying the whole way. When I got in the driveway at home, I got out and kissed the ground. Of course, everybody kept a set of snow-chains in the back of their car, but I didn't think of that.

My dad was so good at driving in snow. I've been with him before when he was going off our mountain road, and it was so bad, he had to drive down in reverse to hold the car back. Now, that's talent. The only wreck he ever had was when, years later, he bought himself a nice, red, four-wheel-drive truck. Coming from town, he decided to try it out because the roads were bad. He slid in a straight spot and flipped it on its top. He blamed the four-wheel-drive. He was probably right because he had never had a vehicle with it before. I don't think he's had one since.

Dad always said that mom didn't drive a car...she herded one. The faster she chewed, the faster she went. Maybe that's why she loved teaching us. Sometimes, she would let us on the hood at the bottom of the mountain, and we would hold onto the wipers while she drove on home. I still did this when I got older, but only on side roads.

It seems odd now to get in a car and have it run so quietly that you can't even hear it. There's a button for everything. There are no dimmer switches in the floor board and no window cranks. Instead of wind blowing through your hair from the window, there's an air conditioner vent aimed just where you want it. The cars we learned to drive are now classics and only seen mostly in car shows. Who would have thought that the car that bounced and burned rubber over the rough, back, country roads would someday be a jewel?

Annie

CHAPTER 1

The sun was hot today. So hot, it stung like one of Momma's switches across my shoulders. Looking up, I didn't see a cloud in sight. Giving the ground another chop with my hoe, I glanced sideways to see how far ahead Momma and Dad were. The big field of corn was just above my knees. It was easy to see they were way- ahead of me. Dust blew in the light breeze every time the three blades hit the ground to cut a weed and draw dirt around the roots. It was at times like these that I wished I had some big, strong brothers like Ruby Mae Dupplin, one of Annie's closest friends, had. The rocky dirt was as hot as fresh stove ashes under my feet. My thin, cotton dress stuck to my body like you had dipped me in water. Sometimes, I figured it made my dad mad that Momma had only given him two daughters. Sons could have worked harder; there would have been less for him to worry about. But two girls are what he got, and Ginny had run off and married Nathan, the first boy that had winked at her when she was fourteen. Maybe when I turn fourteen in a few years, I can do the same. Coming to the end of my row, a while later, I could see them resting in the shade of the big chestnut tree. My dad stood tall, a little on the thin side. Leaning against the tree, he fanned his face and head with his battered old hat. Momma sat on a rock, drinking water, barely cool now, from the dipper. Dropping it back in the bucket, she leaned her head back against the tree to catch the breeze around her neck. I could tell Dad wouldn't be too happy with my work by the look he gave me as I propped my hoe next to theirs. Squatting down, I drank half of the water, then lifted the dipper and let the rest run in slow, warm trails down my head.

"Don't waste that water, Annie, unless you want to walk back to the spring and refill that bucket."

"Okay, Dad," I mumbled as I sat down beside Momma. Turning her head to me, she gave a half, weak grin. Her eyes seemed to say, 'Nevermind him.' Every time he moved, I flinched, thinking it was time to start back. Between the buzzing of the bees and the birds chirping, my eyes started getting heavy. Dad must have noticed, and not wanting us to get too comfortable, he grabbed his hoe and started walking. 'Lord, help us,' I thought as I followed them to the start of a new row. Soon, the hoes could be heard echoing down through the woods that surrounded our house. Momma hummed to herself; Dad grunted every now and then. And I let my mind drift to my sister, Ginny. After she ran off, she wrote Momma a letter and said they had settled next to Nathan's grandpa's farm. Nathan's grandparents were letting them use the old cabin they had before they built the small clapboard house they now lived in. Months had passed now. 'I wonder if she is going to have a baby,' I thought. That would be wonderful! Maybe I could even go sometimes and help her with it. Smiling, I hoed with a flutter of excitement in my belly. But unless she wrote to us, we would probably never know. Dad had sworn he would take the hide off of her for running off when he saw her again. It could be a while before she comes back around...if she does. But I could dream, so I dreamed big as I made my way out the row of corn.

The day dragged on. Finally, I heard my dad holler, "I reckon we'll quit now." Dad took the thin, red handkerchief out of his back pocket and wiped his forehead. It looked like a flag of surrender blowing in a gentle whiff of air. He stuffed the rag back into his pocket. 'Bout time,' I thought to myself, walking with Momma back to the house. Dad shuffled slowly towards the barn to put the hoes away and take care of the milk cow.

"Momma, can I go soak my feet in the creek for a bit and cool off some?"

"Sure. Go ahead, Annie, but don't stay too long. Your dad likes everybody at the table when he sits."

"I won't," I whispered, grinning at her. Shaking her head, she turned and went into the house. Taking off, I started down the path leading to the creek in a quick walk. "If it wasn't for the work, I might just like summer." This time, I spoke out loud. Only the squirrels and birds could hear you down here. Looking up as I walked, I could see the blue sky through the canopy of the poplars and pine trees. The path was worn smooth from the many trips Ginny and I had made. Ever so often, a tree root or rock would disrupt the smooth dirt.

I could hear the water before I saw it, a rolling, tumbling sound. Rocks, both big and small, scattered the creek bank. Tying my skirt tail higher up my legs, I waded into the cold, rushing water. Letting my toes sink into the gritty sand, I closed my eyes and smiled as the water lapped at my legs. The coolness of the water reminded me of a time long ago, when I had to make a trip to the town doctor.

My throat had been so swollen, I couldn't even get a sip of cold water down. Momma had tried everything, even that yucky groundhog-grease, but nothing worked. Finally, they wrapped me in a quilt. After borrowing an old truck from Buster, a family friend, they dropped Ginny off at Grandma's, then went on to town with me. After removing my tonsils, which had been badly infected, I was allowed to leave after staying the night. On the way out of town, Dad had stopped at the only drug store the town had to get the medicine the doctor had prescribed.

"Be back in a jiff, honey," Momma had said. Nodding, I watched as she opened the squeaky truck door, then disappeared through the shiny glass door into the drug store.

"She'll be right back. Don't worry," Dad had said, speaking in a matter-of-fact voice. My mouth slid into a painful grin. Looking at him, I had known that he felt better with her around too. Not long after, the door had swung open, and Momma had come walking back to the truck, medicine in one hand and a vanilla cone in the other.

"Here, honey, I got you a little treat for being such a big girl," she had said, giving me a smile. I had felt Dad chuckle a little beside me as I reached for the cone. Looking ahead, he started the truck while Momma made sure it was clear to pull out. I had taken small, savoring licks as the truck bounced along the road, heading out of town towards home. Now, the cold water reminded me of that ice cream.

Smiling to myself, I let the memory slip away and gave in. Sitting down in the water, it went up to my armpits. Leaning over, I dunked my whole head under. Running my fingers through my hair, I let the water wash away the dust and heat of the day. It was down here at the creek that I had told Ginny all the wonderful things I had seen in town. Trucks and cars. Everybody had shoes on, and the girls had worn dresses with buttons halfway down their back. Shiny store windows. Ladies carrying brown paper bags, not boxes, of groceries. Gosh... I missed talking to Ginny. No wonder Ginny had ran off. There was a whole new world out there, just below the mountains. All we had was a little country store that was part of old man Hanes' house and a church that overlooked the cemetery, which held the good, the bad, the young, and the old. During the weeks, five months out of the year, it was our school.

It was no secret around here that the biggest reason people didn't go to town was because a lot of the men were moonshiners. Dad made most of his living making hat-racks. He was good, and he sold quite a few. But we all knew what the corn was for. He didn't actually make whiskey, but he sold the corn to make it.

Looking around, I could see that the shadows had gotten deeper. Not wanting to be late, I stood and wrung the water from my dress and hair. Giving everything a quick shake, I started walking back to the house. I sat down just as dad stepped into the house. Our house was as modest as the rest of the homes in Piney Holler. It was made of boards split from the trees off of our land and had a loft for the children, one bedroom for Momma and Dad, and then the kitchen, which served as both the sitting down room and the kitchen.

There Momma stood, one hand on her hip, the other finishing the cornmeal gravy. Dad was buttering a piece of cornbread while he waited for her to finish and sit down. Cold buttermilk from the spring sat in glasses that were sweating from the heat of the cook stove. Everybody's but mine, that is. I couldn't stand the taste, so Momma had plain, creamy, white milk in mine.

"Come on, Lois. I'm starving here," said Dad's impatient voice.

"Hold your horses, Cecil," Mom answered, rolling her eyes.

After setting the gravy on the table, Momma wiped her face with the apron around her waist. Taking a quick look around, she made sure she had everything before sitting down herself.

"Okay, Annie, say the blessing before your dad starves." Momma grinned across the table at him.

"Yes, Momma." So, I blessed the food, then gave Dad a look that said, 'Dive in.'

Dad spooned gravy onto the cornbread with one hand while the other hand speared a fat piece of fried pork.

"I'm glad to see you took a bath while you were down at the creek." Momma waited for my reply.

"Well...sorta," I replied, grinning sheepishly.

By then, we were all busy spooning Momma's delicious food into our stomachs. The light off the sun, which was going down, glared through all six panes of glass in the window. I couldn't help but glance at Ginny's empty chair. 'Surely, she'll get in touch soon,' I thought as I let the cool milk wash down my throat.

"So..." Momma started, speaking to me but looking at Dad. "How bout you and me have a day off tomorrow and go find some raspberries for a pie?" Eyes bright, she turned and looked at me.

"I'm ready!" I answered, looking at her with excitement in my eyes.

"Okay, little girl, tomorrow it is. That okay with you, Cecil?" Momma asked as she stood to pour Dad a cup of coffee to finish off his meal.

"Fine with me; I've got to finish some things in the barn anyway."

Looking at each other, Momma and I both smiled real big, excited to have a plan for a fun day. Later that evening, as darkness draped the mountains, Dad sat on the porch in a cane-bottom chair, whittling away as cedar shavings gathered at his feet in golden ribbons. Momma had lit the oil lamp, and now she sat on the porch, reading from the family Bible, as she did every night. Climbing the ladder to the loft, I sat on the foot of the bed, looking out past the white birch tree that seemed to be standing guard, limbs stretched in every direction. Picking up the hairbrush, I began brushing the knots out of my hair before bed. The humm of Dad and Momma's voices could be heard coming from the porch. Standing, I stretched my arms and arched my back. The day's work was slowly wearing me down, and my bed was looking pretty comfy. Pulling my thin, cotton, summer nightgown over my head, I descended the ladder to make my nightly trip to the outhouse before bed. Dad had rolled a smoke, and the flaming, red-yellowish glow could be seen at the end of the porch.

"All ready for bed, sweetie?" Momma asked. I could only see half of her from the glow of the oil lamp shining from the kitchen window.

"As soon as I go to the outhouse, I will be," I said, yawning.

"Well, me and Dad will sit here and wait for you before we go in, okay?"

"Okay," I said, and 1 hopped off the porch. Even in the night, my feet took no time finding the familiar path across the yard, which led to the edge of the barn lot. Dad's sweet tobacco smoke drifted gently in the night breeze. The evening air was cool, and not a single sound could be heard except the soft song of the little frogs along the path leading to the creek. Would I or would I not miss this place if I ever left? I stopped in the path. Closing my eyes, I let the silent beauty of the night take me away for a moment.

"Don't dilly-dally, Annie." Dad's voice broke the stillness.

It was darker than a poke full of black cats in the outhouse. It was my fault though; I should have at least brought a candle. I made short work of my business and hurried back, slowing as I neared the porch.

"Little out of breath, ain't you, Annie?" Dad asked, chuckling.

"Well, it's darker down there," I answered, defending myself.

"Come on. Give us some sugar, and get in the bed," Momma said, laughing. I gave Dad a quick peck on the forehead, and I gave Momma one on the cheek. Inside, I headed up the ladder to the loft.

Climbing into bed, I let the cotton mattress and feathered pillow cuddle me from head to toe. The deep and throaty hoot of an owl was the last sound I heard.

I woke the next morning to the sound of the stove lids banging as Momma fixed breakfast. Hurriedly, I dressed in the oldest stained dress I had for the berry picking. At my last step on the ladder, I quickly let Momma know that I was on my way to the chicken coop to gather the eggs before she could get the reminder out of her mouth. 'I love doing this to her,' I thought. It was the kind of game we played when we were excited to hurry and do something fun. If one of us had to remind the other to do something important, that person lost points. Coming to a stumbling stop in the doorway, I grinned at Momma and said, "Don't forget to heat my syrup." Laughing, I flew onto the porch and out into the dewy grass. Momma was left with an 'I can't believe you got me' look on her face.

Everything was in a full uproar down at the chicken coop. Roosters were crowing, and hens were a'clucking. They greedily gathered around my feet as I threw the feed in a circular pattern. While the chickens were busy feasting, I quickly felt each nest for the eggs. After finishing, I closed the chicken-wire gate and headed back to the house. As soon as we had eaten breakfast and cleaned up, Momma gave Dad a peck on the cheek, and out the door we went. Passing the barn, Momma grabbed a couple of pails for the berries.

"Momma?" I stopped and looked up at her. Turning around, she looked at me.

"Something you want, Annie?" she asked.

"Well.... I was kinda wondering...if Dad's so grumpy, why are you always giving him little pecks on the cheek or forehead?" I asked.

"Come on." She smiled, putting her arm around me and swinging the buckets in the other hand as she led me down the path to the field. A few steps later, she continued.

"Annie, honey, I've known your dad for many years. That's just his way."

"To be grouchy all the time?" I asked.

"No." She paused. "Your dad is just a serious man, quiet, a little backwards, and very shy," she said, defending him. "He loves us all very much. He just has a hard time showing it. Now, hush, and let's go get them berries before an old, furry bear does." She laughed.

Maybe she was right. I smiled to myself. "You know what, Momma? Sometimes, you remind me of a little girl."

"You know what, Annie? Sometimes, I feel like one." Together, we went skipping lightly over the path and soon came to the barbed-wire fence. Giggling like two best friends, Momma held the bottom strand of wire up while I crawled under, and then I held the top one down while she crossed over and tried not to get her dress caught up. Following an old cow trail, we scanned the area for some berry briers. The wild flowers were just waking up to catch the sun...black-eyed susan's, bright red and orange poppies, and my favorite, the bachelor-buttons. Men wore those in the button holes of their suit coats or shirts when they were courting. Unlike Ginny, I would make sure my 'Bo' wore one for everybody to see... when I got old enough, that is. It was mid July, and the plants and fruits were showing off. Even the Ben-Davis apples were showing their bright shades of green and red. Slowing to a stop, Momma looked around.

"Okay, Annie, you pick above me on them briers, and I'll pick right here below you on this one. Here...take this stick, and tap the bush some to run any snakes off before you start." Reaching out, I took the dead tree limb.

"If you hear me scream, Momma, you'll know what happened."

"No... If I see you running like a haint, I'll know," she said, laughing.

"Not funny," I joked.

Stepping off the cow trail, I had only taken a few steps when I felt the familiar sharp, hot pain as the brier buried itself into the heel of my foot. Of course, I came to an abrupt stop, hissing and mumbling under my breath. Sitting down,

I pulled my foot up to my face and searched for the painful intruder.

"Momma," I called, not even looking up.

"Yeah, what is it?" she answered, not far away.

"I got a stupid brier in my foot, first thing," I answered her.

"Good Lord, Annie. Couldn't you wait a little longer?"

She walked over to me and squatted down to look at my foot.

"No, I figured it would feel so good, so I just decided to go ahead and get it over with," I answered impatiently.

With a chuckle, she fished around in her dress pocket, bringing out a worn, brown, leather change purse. Snapping it open, she gently brought out a shiny sewing needle, a red piece of thread hanging from it.

"Holy cow, Momma! You carry a needle around with you? What for?" I asked.

"Annie, a momma is always prepared." She took my foot in her hand.

Leaning back on both hands, I turned my head a little, squinting my eyes closed, and waited for the first prick of the needle. Peeping, I could see Momma's shimmering, red head bent in determination to rid me of the pesky brier.

"Ouch, Momma!" I shrieked. Tightening her grip, she held onto my foot to keep it still.

"Hold still, Annie. I've just about got it," she cautioned.

Leaning forward, I watched as Momma, with the tip of the needle, brought the brier slowly out of my foot. I flopped back on the ground in relief. Looking around at me, Momma's laugh rang through the pasture.

"Let me help you up, you poor baby." Still laughing, she held her hand out to me, grunting as she straightened up off her knees, pulling me along.

"Wait," Momma said as she dusted her dress off. "I got something I want to show you."

"What is it, Momma?" I gushed. With a sneaky look on her face, she eased her hand back into her pocket, retrieving a wrinkled, brown envelope. I knew what it was before she opened her mouth. Both my hands covered my mouth, my eyes now wide with excitement.

"Come over here out of them briers and sit beside me." Her voice was shaky now, but her face glowed. Unable to believe it, I sat down beside her, my insides jumping all around now. Taking my hand down from my mouth, I dared to ask, "Is that from Ginny?" My voice was hopeful. Looking at the folded letter, she nodded. Taking a deep breath to calm her shaking hands, she looked at me steadily.

"What does it say?" I couldn't control myself any longer.

"Listen, Annie, you can't open your mouth about this to anyone, not even Ruby Mae, okay?" She waited.

"Oh, Momma, I promise I won't!"

"Alright then." Unfolding the letter, she began to read.

> *Dear Momma,*
>
> *I hope this letter finds you well. I just had to let you know that I'm doing fine and learning as I go. Nathan is so good to me. He brings me flowers almost every day. You and Annie would really like him. He can tell the funniest tales and jokes you ever heard! Nathan's mom, Frances, is teaching me the secrets to cooking. I could burn water.*

Momma and I both laughed at this, and then she continued reading.

But I'm learning. I have to cause we'll soon have another mouth to feed. There...I said it, and I know you and Annie are just a'busting wide open!

And, yes, we were. Tears were dripping from Momma's cheeks. "Hurry and finish it, Momma!" I couldn't wait another second.

"Okay, okay, hush now." Her hand swiped at the moisture on her face, and she began reading again.

Anyway, I love you all, and I hope Daddy will break down and let me visit soon. I really want you with me, Momma, when my time comes. I'll send word if I don't get to see ya. Be good, Annie. I miss you.
Love,
Ginny

Both our heads were still bent over, looking at the letter. My arms hugged my knees to me. Raising my head, I watched as Momma folded the letter as neatly as a bed sheet. "Will you talk to Daddy, Momma?"

With wisps of hair dancing around her face, she smiled at me, looking determined. "Indeed, I will. It's about time your daddy got over this little mad spell of his, and I'm about fed up with it too."

Grinning from ear to ear, I jumped to my feet, ready to run back to the house.

"Hold on, now. We got to ease into this, little girl. Butter him up and stuff." She laughed, getting up too.

"Now, the way to a man's heart is through his stomach. That's what my momma always said. So, we're going to pick the berries, take a few of those ripe apples, and commence to sweetening up your daddy. We'll make a raspberry pie first."

Momma was all excited now, hands a'going every which way. She pinned her loose hair back up, bobby-pins clutched between her teeth. "Then, we'll hit him with a yummy apple-sauce cake! He'll never see it coming." She winked at me. By now, I was all fired up too! "Now, get back up there on them briers, and get to picking while I get these down here," she ordered.

"Yes, ma'am!" And up I went, stepping carefully this time. I didn't want any more interruptions. My thoughts were racing, and my hands were shaking with excitement, but somehow, I managed to hold steady and began filling my pail with the berries. A lone cow mooed from way down in the pasture, her big cow-bell clanging along with her slow, shuffling steps. Bees buzzed around, hunting a sweet taste of juice. The little black ants ran around in a tiff because their ant-hills were being disturbed. Momma could be heard humming "Buffalo Gals (Won't You Come Out Tonight?)," her soft voice meeting with the sounds from the old milk cows. The earthy breeze swept across the fields and mountain. Holding my hand over my eyes, I squinted against the sun as I looked to see how far she had gone. She was almost back at the fence now.

"I'm all done up here, Momma!" I hollered.

"Me too," she answered as she waved me down to her. Holding on tightly to my pail, I eased my way back down to her. Holding the pail out to her, she took it and began picking the trash out of it...a leaf, a stem, some green berries.

"I got almost a half of a pail, Momma."

"Me too. That will be plenty enough for a pie, or even a cake." She smiled as she poured mine into her pail. "Now, let's go over there to the apple tree and get us a few ripe ones. Have to be prepared for our plan," she whispered sneakily. Laughing,

I grabbed her hand, and off we went, crossing back over and under the fence.

Reaching the apple tree, we searched the ground for 'falls.' They would be riper. Holding my dress tail up, I made a pouch to hold my apples while Momma carried the pail. It didn't take long to find what we needed. Sitting in the shade of the tree, we each picked a good, ripe apple that only had a few bruises, and we sunk our teeth into them, the juice running from the apples onto our chins.

"Mmmm, Annie," Momma said in a savory voice. "This hits the spot...a little piece of heaven right here on earth."

"Yep," I answered. "These will make a pie that will melt in your mouth," I sputtered as I took another bite.

Throwing the cores down the hill, we gathered up our harvest of fruit and headed back on the path towards home.

"Now, remember, Annie, control your excitement around your daddy. Don't let the cat out of the bag before we get started."

"My lips are sealed, Momma. Nobody could drag it out of me."

"Just act as normal as always. Don't even mention Ginny's name, okay?" Momma spoke low into my ear.

"I won't let you down, Momma. You'll be so proud of me." I smiled up at her.

"Come on, you silly girl." Momma chuckled. "I love you, Annie."

"Love you too, Momma."

CHAPTER 2

Momma waited till the next day after breakfast, when Daddy went to work in the barn. Then, she announced we were ready to start our 'buttering up' on Daddy.

Out on the table, she arranged all the ingredients for the pie crust while the berries simmered on the stove, sweetened to perfection.

"Let me get all this mixed up and ready, and then you can do the honors of rolling it out nice and thin for me. Okay, Annie?"

"I'm ready, Momma. Done washed my hands and all!" I answered, ready to get rolling. Her hands scooped, pinched, and dashed the ingredients into the mixing bowl. Then, she flopped the dough onto the table and kneaded it until it passed her inspection.

"Now, Annie, dash you a little flour on the table in front of you, and then rub some on the rolling pin." Momma placed the wad of dough in the flour. With my knees in the chair, I was in a good position to bear down on the fluffy white dough with the heavy rolling pin. Up and down, back and forth I went while Momma stirred and tasted the filling. Then, she placed the pie pans in the oven to heat up to be greased.

"Looking good," Momma said as she looked over her shoulder at me with her eyebrows raised. With a little praise, I forgot my tired arms and attacked the dough again. Momma made it look so easy when she did it, but the roller got heavier and heavier to me.

"Okay, now..." Momma's voice held a hint of mischief. "We are ready to place the crust in the pan and tuck those delicious berries inside."

Gladly, I laid the rolling pin down. Momma eased her hands under the dough, lifting it up gently and placing it over the pan. Next, she pressed the dough all around the inside of the pan. Then, taking a knife, she trimmed the edges.

"Momma, can I take the fork and put the crinkles all around the edge?" I asked.

"Sure. Here's you a fork. Start this one while I fix the other one." Handing me the fork, she dusted off her hands and started placing the dough in the next pie pan. Soon, they were done, covered nice and neat with the top crust on and the bird's foot cut daintily into the center of each one. Streams of steam from the pie filling inside came up through the little slices in the top crust. Opening the oven door, Momma gently placed each pie inside. Next, she lifted the lid where the wood went to make sure the coals and flame were just right.

"Now, we'll clean up this mess while they bake. I'll fix some wash water in the pan, and you can be washing a few dishes while I put all the evidence up and sweep."

Soon, the brown, hot, crusty pies were cooling on the table. The window was open, a cool breeze moving the sweet aroma all over the house. When Dad came in for his midday snack, his eyes fell on the table, and he took in the pies and the sweet juices of the raspberries oozing from the crust.

"What's this, girls?" he asked curiously.

"Oh...we just thought that with all the hard work you've been doing, we should fix a treat for you." Momma smiled, giving him a peck on the cheek. "Now, let's all sit down and enjoy a piece while it's still warm. Annie made the crust too!" She turned to get the saucers and forks while I poured Dad a cup of coffee.

Momma and I sat quietly, watching Dad out of the corners of our eyes, silently smiling inside as we watched him wolf down the slice of pie. It was delicious. Momma could bake a rock and make it taste good. They both had something they were really good at. Momma could cook like no other woman on the mountain, and Dad could take a piece of wood and make things come to life. Almost every business in town owned one of his hat or coat racks, desks, or dish cupboards. Me...well, I hadn't found my talent yet...unless it was being a really good climber. Dad said I was like a squirrel...and just as fast too.

Looking around the table, I could see that Momma and Dad were chitchatting about this and that as they gazed out the window. I sat quietly, wondering when Momma was going to ease in something about Ginny. Swinging my legs under the table, I waited. Momma thoughtlessly twirled a strand of hair around her finger as she talked. Leaning forward, Dad got a serious look on his face as he looked down past the barn at the road. Standing, Momma looked too. Of course, I climbed higher in my chair so I could see. You could see the dust coming up off the road in thin clouds.

"Wonder who that could be?" Dad asked absentmindedly.

Momma untied her apron and laid it across the back of her chair, smoothing her hair as she followed Dad to the front door. Me...I stayed where I was. That way, I had a full view of everything without being asked to sit still. It took a minute or two before the humm of the motor could be heard nearing the back of the barn and coming on up to the edge of the yard. By now, my parents were standing on the porch, waiting. The Ford truck came to a gentle stop as the wind blew the dust back down the hill. Dad slowly went down the three porch steps, hands in his pockets, while Momma waited by the door.

The blue door of the truck opened. The first thing I noticed was the well-rounded belly that was held in by a wide pair of black suspenders. 'No one I ever saw,' I thought as I looked at the chunky, round face of the man who was squeezing out from behind the steering wheel. Reaching back into the truck, he pulled out a worn, black, leather satchel.

"Good afternoon, Mr. Shelton!" the man said. The small, high voice didn't match the robust man.

"Afternoon," Dad mumbled. "Are you lost, sir?"

"No, no, I'm not lost." The man chuckled, wiping his forehead with a white handkerchief. "I have some business to talk over with you, Mr. Shelton, if you care to give me a bit of your time."

"What kind of business?" Dad answered back, still blocking the path to the porch.

"I must say, it's rather sad, but it will hopefully be beneficial to you also. My name is Vernan Wilkes. I'm an attorney from town, and I came to talk to you on behalf of your uncle Jim." he stated.

"What's wrong with Jim that he couldn't come himself?" Dad questioned.

"I'm sorry to say, Mr. Shelton, that your uncle passed the day before yesterday." Mr. Wilkes looked down at the ground in respect before looking back up at Dad. Turning around, Dad looked back up on the porch at Momma. Seeing that he was taken aback some, she smiled and motioned to Mr. Wilkes. "Come on in out of the heat, Mr. Wilkes. I just baked a nice pie, and you and Cecil can sit down while you talk." Stepping aside, Dad let the man pass before following behind him. By the time they came to the table, I was sitting like a little lady.

"Annie, would you care to cut Mr. Wilkes a piece of pie?" Momma asked as she pulled out the chairs for them. Politely, I got up to get the pie while the three settled themselves around the table. Mr. Wilkes began opening the satchel and brought out some papers. I waited, pie in hand, while he situated everything. Finally, the whiff of pie hit his nose, and he turned, giving me a big grin.

"Thank you, little lady." His pudgy fingers reached for the plate.

"You're welcome." I smiled back and went to stand at the sink.

"Now, as I was saying, Mr. Shelton..."

"Just call me Cecil," Dad interrupted.

"Okay, Cecil. As I was saying, your uncle Jim passed away, and he left me in charge of his estate...or property, you might say. Also, as you know, he owned the little corner store on the far end of town. Very profitable little business too!" Dad listened with no emotion, hands folded on the table. "Having no children and his wife passing some years back, he had to find somebody to leave his belongings and business to." Mr. Wilkes paused, looking at Dad and Momma while placing a large bite of pie into his mouth. "Mmmm, Mrs. Shelton, this is heavenly." he breathed.

"Thank you kindly, Mr. Wilkes," Momma said, beaming.

"Anyways, Cecil, I am here to notify you that he has left all his property and belongings to you." He now spoke low and soft to Dad.

All three of us looked like somebody who had walked up on a bear in the woods. Dad was watching his hands like he'd never seen them before. Mom, like a good wife, sat there, waiting for her husband to speak. I had so many things running around in my head that I felt kind of dizzy. Mr. Wilkes shoved pie in his mouth while we all looked bewildered. Finally, Dad spoke.

"So, what do I do, Mr. Wilkes?" Dad's voice was still flat and emotionless.

"Well..." Mr. Wilkes felt around in his shirt pocket until he found a fountain pen. "You just sign these here papers, Cecil, and everything is settled." There was a long pause. Mr. Wilkes used this time to finish off his coffee. Then, he held the pen out to Dad. I could have sworn I saw my Dad's hand shake a little as he took it. He looked over at Mom, as if for her approval, and she gave a small nod. He signed the papers lying in front of him. Laying the pen down, he rubbed his hands back and forth on his pant legs to get rid of the sweat.

"Very well then," Mr. Wilkes stated in a breathy voice. He started shuffling and straightening papers. Giving them a tap on the table, he handed them to Dad. Smiling, he stood and held his hand out for Dad to shake. The legs of Dad's chair made a sound of wood scraping against wood as he stood and pushed the chair back with his legs. Then, they shook hands.

Mr. Wilkes reached deep into the pocket of his pants and pulled out a slim piece of leather that had some keys tied onto it. "Here you go, Cecil. These go to the store, the truck, and the out-building behind the store. Don't know about the other two; you can figure that out later. Now, the store will need immediate attention. A lot of folks depend on it for credit till they get paid. Your uncle was always good to folks that way. So, if you need any help once you get down there, just let me know, and I'll get Ray White to kinda give you a hand till you get the hang of things. He spent a lot of time there keeping Jim company." Gently, he pushed his chair back under the table. "Also, you may want to know that your uncle was given a nice, quiet funeral like he had asked for."

"Thank you...and I'll do that," Dad replied. Mr. Wilkes tipped his hat to Momma and then turned to smile at me.

"I'm sure you will like the school in town, Annie, and you'll make lots of new friends. Good day to you all."

We all walked outside to watch the lawyer leave. He threw his hand out the window to wave as the truck went back down the old dirt road. Now, I felt like I could sit down, so I sat on the first step going off the porch. My legs were weak. I was confused about the man's words. I could hear Dad's shoes dragging as he walked back and forth on the porch behind me. Finally, Momma's voice broke the silence.

"So, what do we do now, Cecil?" Momma sounded bewildered by all the news. Dad sat in his chair and rolled a smoke. Lighting it, he let a long cloud of smoke leave his lungs as he looked at Momma.

"Well, Lois, I guess we're moving to town." Now, Momma sat down, hands wringing in her lap. Dad continued.

"Don't seem like I have a choice. Boy, he sure knows how to dump a load in a man's lap. That's for sure. You heard him. The store can't stay closed long. We'll pack up the valuables first. Then, after we get settled, we'll come back for the rest." He flicked the ashes out into the yard and looked out over the land. For some reason, my eyes got watery. I wasn't sure I wanted to leave now. All of a sudden, town didn't seem so rosy to me...and what about Ginny? If you ask me, that pie sure brought more of a mess than happiness. One minute, we were buttering Dad up, and the next minute, we're leaving the whole place behind! How would she know where to find us? I felt Momma's hand touch the top of my head and give me a pat. I didn't even look up.

"Well, I guess there's nothing else we can do. What's done is done, and now we have a responsibility to Jim." Momma's voice wobbled.

"Come on, girls, it might not be that bad. Annie can go to school and have nice things, and you will have all those little luxuries you've always wanted, Lois." Dad smiled, giving Momma a poke.

"I would still miss this place though, Cecil. Don't know if I'd like living around a lot of people."

"Honey, there ain't that many people in town. We all came from the same bunch of poor folks. Some just got uppity." Dad chuckled. 'Well, this is weird,' I thought. 'I don't think I've seen Dad in this good of a mood since he won forty dollars off of Henry Buck in a poker game that one time.'

"What do you think, Annie?" Momma asked softly. I looked up at both of them, and all of a sudden, I didn't care what I said.

"I want to know how Ginny will find us." My voice quivered.

Both were quiet for a minute, and then Dad cleared his throat. "I've been thinking on that too, Annie, and as soon as we get to town, I'll have your momma write and tell her where we're at." Momma and I smiled at each other like it was Christmas morning.

"You really mean it, Dad?" I jumped up excitedly.

"Yes, I'm serious, Annie, but I'm still going to give them a talking to!" he stated firmly. But we didn't care...it was a start!

"Well, holy cow, let's get packing!" I shouted. Momma and Dad couldn't help but laugh now. "Oh, and by the way, Lois, I don't plan on selling our land just yet. A fellow never knows when he might need it to fall back on."

"Now, I do feel better," Momma gushed, hugging Dad. "I better get some supper on, and then we can plan out what we're going to take and leave for now and what to do with the chickens and things." Momma stood and headed for the stove to start cooking. I took off to get some more firewood, and Dad went to milk the cow.

After supper, Dad walked around outside, looking and pondering, I guess, on what he was going to do with the things he wouldn't be taking. Momma looked over everything in the house over and over again. Me...I sat in my room, glad I didn't have that much to worry about taking. I was just so excited that Ginny would be forgiven and that I could see her any time.

Eventually, we all ended up on the porch again as the sun was going down.

"I think we'll give the chickens to your momma, Lois. The cow will probably come with us for milk and butter." Dad looked over at Momma for a reply.

"Yeah, she would love that." Momma seemed far away.

"I'll get Buster to come by every once in a while to check the place and clean the spring house." Dad's voice seemed to trail off, and Momma just nodded.

Lying in bed that night, my thoughts went to Ruby and all my other friends and family here. Town girls were stuck up and didn't like to get dirty or play in the creek. Why...I bet they wouldn't even pick up a crawfish or worm. All of a sudden, I felt lonely. There would be no more corn shucking, molasses boiling, or pie contests. The branches of the birch tree tapped against my window. In the distance, the low grumble of thunder could be heard. A storm was coming, and soon, the sky was crying as if it was sad to see us go.

The next few days were a blur. Family came over to help. Dad got Buster to drive him into town to get Uncle Jim's truck to haul our stuff. It seemed odd to have a truck of our own, but Dad was as happy as a May fly. Ruby and I promised to keep in touch and spend the night with each other from time to time. Our last night at home was sad. We sat around like we were at a funeral. Then, down through the trees, we could see lights bobbing in the darkness.

"What in the world?" Momma stood, looking harder. We heard them talking before we saw them...Uncle James, Aunt Dot, all the cousins, and a few neighbors. Each of the women carried a pot or covered dish of food. Howdy's and hugs were exchanged. Momma helped take the food in while Dad and the men sat down in chairs or on the porch edge.

"Now, I know y'all have probably done ate, but this will be a little something to heat up in the morning before you head out," Aunt Dot announced.

My cousins and I took off in the dark to catch lightning bugs. Tom, Ruby Mae's dad, brought out his fiddle and started plucking the strings while Aunt Dot hummed to the tune.

I hadn't had so much fun in a long time. We ended up dipping into the food some, and soon after, everybody headed home to tuck the little ones into bed. I was too tired to lay awake and think, and I soon fell asleep.

The next morning, we ate the leftovers from the night before, cleaned up, and started loading the truck. Soon, Momma's family came walking up the path to help. Dad didn't have any close family. He was an only child, and his mom and dad had died when their cabin caught fire from a piece of stove wood that had rolled out of the fireplace late one night while they slept. I was two when that happened. Uncle Jim and a few distant aunts were all he had besides me and Momma.

Grandma hugged me and nearly kissed my face off, telling me to be a good girl and not to let the town kids fool me into anything bad.

"Leave her alone, Nolie. They might have 'town-smarts,' but Annie has 'hill-skills'" Grandpa said, giving a toothless laugh and pulling my hair gently.

"Oh, hush, you old goat," Grandma grumbled. The chickens were squawking in their crates, ready to go to Grandma's. The truck was loaded down, and soon, everybody was hugging us bye. Aunt Dot, Momma's brother James, and all the kids stood in the yard and waved as we started down the yard and then on down the road. Sitting between Momma and Dad, I started feeling a little excited.

"Here we go, girls. And don't worry... we'll be spending our Sunday mornings at Piney Hill Free Will Baptist, okay?" Dad let out a long breath, and the truck went bumping along.

"Thanks, Cecil." Momma smiled. Of course, this made me happy too. Even though a lot of the men from home were not without sin, their wives dragged them to church every Sunday, and Dad was one of those men.

CHAPTER 3

The truck was an older model, but it had been well kept. Dad felt like the brakes would need to be replaced before long, but other than that, it was in tip-top shape. I just wanted to see the store and the living quarters, which is what Momma called that part of the house. We passed an old farm and Ruby's house, which sat up on the hill with her Momma's pretty rose bushes hugging the porch. Fence posts lined the road on both sides, marking every man's property and keeping the live stock in. A few mud puddles were left from the rain we had gotten, making little muddy splashes as we passed over them.

We traveled the long and winding mountain road, burning all the familiar scenes into our minds as if we would never return again.

Soon, the road widened and became a little smoother. The fence posts turned into tall poles with wires running from one to another in a lazy loop. Momma sat up a little straighter while Dad shifted the truck into another gear. I knew we were getting close. The houses sat a little closer here, and the farms were smaller. The family dogs ran free in the yards with close-cut grass. Some of them were nice homes, but some were a little shabby looking, with junk lying around the old barns and sheds.

After driving for a while, Dad began slowing the truck down. Taking a left turn, we started down the main road that would lead us through town. This road was wider than the others. Wooden walkways lined both sides in front of the stores. There was a barber shop, a drug store, a post-office, and a doctor's office on one side...along with various other businesses. On the right, there was a cozy little restaurant, which was lit up with neon lights that said 'Bell's Diner' and 'Open.' You could see the red leather that covered the booth seats through the shiny windows. The theater stood tall, and it seemed that every color of light ran in a snake-like pattern all around the advertisements. Brown's clothing store stood plain, but clean and tidy looking, with clothing displayed on window shelves.

Dad slowed the truck, gearing it down, and we all leaned to the left to get our first look at our new home. It stood on the business side of town. Windows trimmed in faded red paint ran from one end of the porch to the other. The red paint made each pane of glass give off a rosy glow in the sun. Cane-bottomed chairs sat haphazardly along the porch, wood shavings scattered around the legs. The floor boards of the porch were worn smooth by years of folks coming and going. The screen door that led into the store was aged, but it was still doing its job.

Nailed to the top of the porch roof was a large, wooden sign with 'Jim's Store' written in weathered, yellow paint. Dad pulled the truck around back and then turned the key off. We all sat in silence and stillness for a minute. Looking at Dad, who was staring out the windshield, I waited for one of them to make the first move.

Momma made the first move. Reaching for the door handle, she opened the door to get out. "Come on," she said to both of us. "Ain't going unload itself." Crawling across the seat, I slid out of the truck to stand beside Momma. My toes curled in the soft dirt under my feet. "Lord, Annie, we're gonna have to get you a pair of shoes to wear," Momma exclaimed.

"It's summer, Momma," I answered, confused.

"Well, you can't go traipsing around barefooted in town," she answered in a huff before helping Dad loosen the ropes across the bed of the truck.

"Let's let this wait till we go in and look around. Let's see what it looks like," Dad suggested.

So, we waited behind Dad as he took the key and unlocked the back door. Groaning a little, the door slowly opened into the kitchen. A small table with benches on each side sat in the center of the room, a chair at both ends. It was as big as our whole downstairs area at our old house! My eyes were as big as saucers. The kitchen had a stove and one of those new electric iceboxes. Well...it was new to me. Both had been gently used over the years. But thank goodness, in the far corner, there was a familiar cook-stove like the one Momma had at home. Windows lined the sink so you could look out as you washed dishes. Jim's wife had made blue checkered curtains for them when she was here, giving it a cozy look.

Momma walked around, letting her hand glide over every-thing as she checked out the main room of the house. Dad wondered into the store area while we looked.

A long curtain at the other corner of the kitchen opened up to a small family room. Two flowery, wingback chairs sat on each side of the small fireplace. A settee was against the back wall under a large window, which had a view of the small yard and a maple tree. A nick-nack shelf held a few books and ceramic figures of wildlife. The floor was partially covered with a worn, but clean carpet to match the chairs.

"Oh, Annie, it's so fancy!" Momma exclaimed, sounding nervous.

"I know, Momma," I breathed, looking around, afraid to move.

"I'm used to just plain living. What will I do with all these things? I don't know how to cook on an electric stove! Why, I'd burn the house down." She chuckled.

"Ah, Momma, it couldn't be that hard. Maybe Ginny knows. She's been around Nathan's momma's things like these. Surely, she's seen how it's done."

"You're right, Annie. We will just have to hurry and get her here in a few days. Together, we can surely figure it out, I hope." Momma laughed at herself. There we stood, laughing into the air, when Dad poked his head in.

"What's so funny?" he asked.

"Oh, nothing. So, what did you find? How does the store look?" Momma asked.

"Well..." Dad started. "He sure wasn't sloppy. Everything's as neat as a pig pen. Looks just about the same as it did when Dad used to bring me here when I was younger. Come on. I'll show you the rest, Lois. You too, Annie. Come on."

As we left the kitchen, a little hall ran down the length of the store. A little door opened up to the washroom. A big, white, porcelain tub and wash stand graced the small room. But the best part was the indoor toilet! I wouldn't have to be scared a snake was going get me when I sat down anymore. A set of stairs went up at the end of the hall, right where the door to the store was.

"We'll go up there later. First, I want you all to see the store," Dad said.

Trailing behind, we followed him into the store. Looking around, it wasn't much different from the store on Piney Hill. There were more dry goods, like shoes and machine-made clothing, and there was a bigger selection of cloth and medicine. The main counter held an adding machine, a cheese cutter, and scales to weigh things, but it was the front of the counter that was breathtaking. Inside the shiny glass were candies of every kind and suckers of every color. It was like a rainbow had landed right there behind the glass. Gold watches and leather billfolds were also kept there to keep the dust off of them.

I could hear Momma and Dad mumbling in the background. Looking up again, my eyes caught the glass canisters sitting on a shelf. They held the gum-drops, stick candy, licorice, and round balls of bubble gum in every flavor. My mouth watered, and then it hit me...it's all ours! Holy cow! Turning around, the words tumbled out of my mouth as I asked Dad, "Can I have a piece, please?" Looking at my excited expression, he laughed.

"Sure, but only three pieces, Annie, okay?"

"Yes, Dad," I answered. Then, I started the nerve-wracking task of picking from all that candy. 'Oh, just wait till Ruby Mae sees this,' I thought. Our store back home had candy, but not like this! Finally, I picked one gumdrop, a chocolate coin, and a piece of purple gum. They tasted heavenly.

"Well, how do y'all like our new home?" Dad asked as we all stood there, eyes roaming slowly around the store. My jaws worked slowly on the gumball as I followed Dad's gaze around the room.

"It just don't seem real," Momma answered. "Everything happened so fast, but I reckon we'll get used to everything."

Dad reached up and took the battered hat off his head. Walking over to the hat-rack, he looked over the new hats hanging there. His hand hung in mid-air. He reached out and took the dark tan hat off its hook, placing it on his head. "If I'm gonna be a storekeeper, I better look the part." He turned and looked at me and Momma.

"Looks good, Cecil." Momma smiled.

'Yep,' I thought. 'I could get used to this.' "Come on, Annie. Let's start unloading the truck," Momma said, nudging me along as she smiled.

CHAPTER 4

It took a few days, but we soon had all of our things from home put in their appropriate places. Upstairs, the bedrooms were right across from each other. Compared to my loft room at home, my new room was large, and I had a dresser with a long, glass mirror and a wardrobe to hang my few dresses and my coat. There were two windows, one looking out to the back and one looking out to the front. I could look at the entire town, sitting up here like a princess in her tower. I hoped that I would soon look out and see Ginny coming down the street. Momma had sent the letter. We waited patiently for her reply.

Ray, the man who had worked at the store with Jim, had been coming by and helping Dad get the feel of things in the store...figuring out who got credit and who didn't, ordering the supplies, and paying the bills. Momma still cooked on the wood stove. She was waiting on Ginny to help her. Momma could be a little timid about some things. Dad had a meeting at the bank the next day to go over the finances of how well the store did and the profits it brought in. Momma bustled around, dusting and sweeping, making sure the windows were shining. Some days, I would sit on the store steps and watch the people come in and out.

There was one lady that came one day with a little boy about my age. You could tell his momma fed him well, but he had the sweetest face and smile. You just couldn't help it... you had to smile at him. I was waiting for them to come out when I heard the screen door shut. Looking back, I saw him walk out, and then he came over to me.

"Hi, my name's Timmy," he said.

"Hi," I answered back, "my name's Annie."

"Did your daddy take over Jim's store after he passed?" he asked, squinting at the sun.

"Jim was my dad's uncle, and he left him the store when he passed," I answered.

"Oh, I see. Well, sorry for your loss," he replied back as he sat down on the step beside me. "My daddy passed two years ago from a weak heart." Timmy's head hung low now.

"I'm so sorry," I said to Timmy.

"Yeah, it's no fun not having a daddy. Momma works at Bell's Diner now to support us. She does pretty good. During the day, I mostly hang out by myself around the house," he said sadly.

"Well, I'm new here, so I don't know anybody...just you now." I laughed. Timmy chuckled too. The screen door shut again. Timmy's mom came out carrying a brown bag of groceries.

"Guess I got to go," he said. My heart sank. Quickly, I thought of something fantastic.

"Ma'am," I said to his mom, "if it's okay with you, and if Timmy wants to, he can come play with me any time he wants." I smiled at her. Timmy looked at her pleadingly.

"You sure it's okay with your mom and dad?" she asked.

"Oh, Momma would be glad to get me out of her hair for a while." I smiled sweetly.

"Well, I guess it's okay then...as long as he behaves!" she stressed.

"I promise, Momma!" Timmy gushed excitedly.

We were both excited now. Saying goodbye, Timmy promised to stop in the next day after his chores. I couldn't wait.

Stepping out onto the store-porch, Momma told me to run and fetch the mail in case Ginny had written. Smoothing my dress, I started down the walkway to the post office. Not many people were out. It really wasn't a busy town. It was kind of laid back, moving like molasses over a biscuit.

In the distance, I could see Ben Bakster leaving the hardware store with a roll of fencing on his shoulder. Other than that, I didn't see anybody.

When I entered the post office, the clerk smiled. He knew why I was here due to the many trips I had made.

"Looks like this is your lucky day, young lady!" He beamed. Reaching behind him, he pulled out the letter from its cubby hole. Leaning over the counter, he smiled and placed it in my hand. At first, I just stared at it. Chuckling, he said, "Must be very important, little lady."

"Oh, yes sir, it is," I answered, finally catching my breath. Giving him a grin and a quick thank you, I rushed out of the door, the little bell chiming as the door shut. I raced down the wooden walkway, my footsteps echoing behind me. When I got back to the store, I went to the back door, where I knew I would find Momma in the kitchen. Sheepishly, I brought my hand from behind my back and held the letter out to her.

"Finally!" she squealed, snatching the letter from my hand.

"Hurry, Momma!"

"I'm trying," she breathed as she ran the knife blade along the top to open it. "Now, sit down, Annie, and we will read it together."

Sitting side-by-side on the bench, heads huddled together, Momma opened the letter.

> *Dear Momma,*
>
> *I was so shocked to hear all the good news you wrote about! Can't believe you all are town people now. Tell Dad I love him and can't wait to come see you all. We should be there on Friday. If it's okay, I'm staying till the baby comes. I don't want to be without you when my time comes. Won't be much longer either. I'll hush now. So excited, I can't stand it! Hugs and kisses. Tell Annie to be ready. She's got a lot of rocking coming her way.*
>
> *Love,*
> *Ginny*

"This Friday!" Momma exclaimed. "We have to get ready, Annie. Make sure the doctor is aware and waiting. We'll have to have the diapers and things ready too."

Momma was standing now, pacing around like a hen scratching for corn.

"Can I run and tell Dad?" I asked.

"Run along, but be calm if there's anybody in the store." she said.

No one was in the store. Somehow, I repeated the whole letter to him in one breath. Dad smiled and nodded as he watched my face.

"Go help your momma while I close up. I gotta get to the bank before it closes, okay?" he answered as he put his new hat on his head.

I ran off to follow his orders and help Momma start the preparations for Ginny and Nathan.

For two days, we cleaned and sewed diapers for the baby. Timmy came by, but instead of playing, he helped me beat the rugs and sweep the backyard. He did such a good job, Dad paid him fifty cents. He jingled the money around in his pocket, walking around like he was six feet tall.

After Momma was content with the supplies, she gave me and Timmy permission to explore some. So, over the next two days, we walked around the nearby farms and followed paths leading to branches and creeks. Timmy showed me the sheriff's office. Old man Tate, otherwise known as Sheriff Bridges, was was a good man, Timmy told me, but he could be tough too. When we got tired of exploring, we played under the oak tree.

Finally, Friday came. I watched from my bedroom window all morning. Around noon, I saw an old, blue Packard coming slowly through the middle of town. 'This has to be her,' I thought. I had never seen that car before. Flying down the stairs, I hollered, "I think she's here, Momma! Go look! Quick! She might be lost!"

Momma dashed out of the back door just in time to see Ginny opening the car door. After flying down the steps, Momma had her arms stretched out before Ginny was even all the way out of the car. Dropping her hands, Momma looked at the bulging front of Ginny's dress and then gently took her in her arms. I wasn't going to miss out, so I wiggled in between them, one arm around Ginny, one around Momma. We hugged and cried until we heard the other car door shut.

Walking around the back of the car was Nathan. He was tall and slim, with hair that was cut short. He had a big, toothy grin covering his face. I had seen him a couple of times when he had come to revival at our church. Then, he had later run off with Ginny.

"Now, you girls better watch it, or you'll squeeze so hard that the baby will just pop right out!" He laughed.

"Oh, Nathan, you silly thang," Ginny answered, wiping her face. Taking his hand, she looked at Momma. "Momma, this is Nathan Calaway, my husband." Ginny smiled lovingly up at him.

"Nice to meet you, Nathan," Momma said, sticking her hand out to shake.

"No, young lady, I get one of those bear hugs, just like she did." Nathan pointed to Ginny and then grabbed Momma in a big hug. "You too, little girl!" He picked me up off the ground in a spin and hugged me tightly. We were all laughing now. No wonder Ginny loved him. He was already a barrel of fun! Dad didn't come out. I knew he saw them come around the store. He was just being Dad. They would have to go to him first. Finally, we made it into the house. Ginny loved it.

The rest of the day was a whirlwind. Nathan eased off into the store to get to know Dad. Us girls talked, giggled, and caught up on all that had happened since we had last seen each other. Momma just couldn't keep her hands off Ginny's belly, trying to reassure herself that the baby was positioned right. She would also look at Ginny's feet to make sure they weren't swollen.

Later, Ginny and I peeled taters while Momma sliced ham to put in the oven for supper. After pouring a dark brown maple syrup over the ham, she placed apple slices all around the edges.

We had made a chocolate cake and cherry pie the day before. It was August now, so fresh green beans and corn were cooking slowly on the cook-stove.

"I think I'll go see what the men are doing while you put the potatoes on, Annie." Ginny stood, stretching her back. I looked at Momma, and we both watched her walk out of the door and into the store.

"Don't worry, Annie. They'll be alright. Nathan would have already come running if your dad hadn't liked him," she said, laughing.

After setting the potatoes on the stove, Momma and I sat and fanned ourselves while we waited on the food to cook. The little, metal, open-faced fan sat on the pie-safe, humming quietly, stirring the warm air like a slow, bubbling soup. At 5:15, Dad, Ginny, and Nathan came back through the door from the store, talking and grinning like nothing had ever happened. I felt all warm inside.

Supper was a humm of voices back and forth across the table. Nathan told us about how he worked at his father's garage, working on cars or anything with wheels. Now, he was taking time off until Ginny had the baby.

"First thing on Monday morning, we will go to Doctor Bailey's office to see what he has to say about you," Momma told Ginny.

"Not a bad idea, Lois," Dad agreed, waving his fork in her direction.

The new mom and dad just grinned at each other, soaking up the attention. Ginny and I discussed names and what color of hair the baby would have...red like mine and Momma's or dark like her's and Dad's. The atmosphere felt like Christmas morning. Later, the men sat on the back porch, their smoke curling up into the night air. Momma, Ginny, and I cleaned the kitchen, and then we took a break to rest in the sitting room. Windows raised, the sheer curtains gently moved in the breeze. Worn out from the trip and all the excitement, Ginny and Nathan went up to bed before we did. I would sleep on the sofa and let them have my room while they visited. It seemed weird not to be sleeping with Ginny though. Finally, Dad came in from the porch. Momma and Dad both kissed me goodnight and went up to bed, turning the lights out on their way.

I laid there in my cozy cocoon, just like a butterfly, happy from the top of my head to the soles of my feet. Having Ginny back around was the greatest! I just wanted the baby to hurry, and it turns out, it didn't take long. After breakfast the next morning, Ginny started feeling uncomfortable in her back and belly. Momma said her time was coming, but it would still be a while.

Timmy came by to visit. Leaving Momma and Ginny to finish getting everything ready for the baby, I went out back to swing and play around the oak tree with him.

"So, is the school here nice, Timmy?" I asked. "I mean, the kids and all," I finished.

"Sure," he answered, dropping to the ground from the low branch of the tree. "Of course, some of the rich kids are snooty, but most are friendly."

"I hope I make some friends. I had lots of them up on the mountain." I looked beyond the town to the mountain as I spoke to Timmy.

"You will, Annie. You're nice...to be a girl," he stated seriously.

Smiling, I released the swing to watch it go around and around.

Around noon, Momma came out and said Ginny wasn't feeling good. If she didn't start feeling better, Momma was going to call the doctor.

"You two play quietly now, and I'll bring y'all a sandwich... and maybe a cold pop too," Momma bargained with us.

"Of course we will, Momma," I answered, looking at Timmy so he would help me reassure her. His head nodded up and down in agreement.

Momma rushed back in the house to make the sandwiches. Timmy looked at me with wide eyes. "Do I need to go home, Annie?" he asked.

"No!" I hurriedly answered, feeling a little scared now. "Stay with me in case we have to run and get help or something."

"Okay, I will," he responded, trying to make his voice sound stout now. "Let's just sit here in the dirt and play with marbles." Reaching into his pocket, he pulled out a fist of colored marbles. After sitting down, we quietly began to play. It wasn't long before Momma came out with the food and drinks. Ginny was lying down. Momma told us the August heat wasn't helping her at all. Momma's forehead was creased with worry. Absentmindedly, she turned and went back into the house without another word. We continued to play while we ate.

Timmy stayed as late as he could. After he left, I went back in the house. Momma was cooking supper.

"Is she okay, Momma?" I asked cautiously.

"Yeah, I reckon. The first one always takes its time." she mumbled.

We all ate silently. Each one of us had our ears open, listening for any sound from upstairs. After we cleaned the dishes, Momma and I went up to check on Ginny.

"Now, listen. If you need me at all in the night, just get Nathan to come and wake me, okay?" Momma was looking at Ginny sternly.

"I will, Momma. I just can't wait till it's over," Ginny answered.

We both gave her a kiss and left the room.

CHAPTER 5

Sometime in the early morning, right before daybreak, I heard footsteps rushing around above me. Momma had hurriedly called Doctor Bailey to come, but no one had answered. In a panic, she pleaded with Dad to go find him. Grabbing his truck keys, he nearly took out the back door in his rush.

Ginny lay upstairs in bed, Nathan holding her hand while Momma wiped her face with a cool rag. I was excited but a little scared when I saw the pain she was in. For some reason, I just wanted to go wait somewhere else until it was over.

Creeping back down the stairs, I decided to wait under the oak tree. That way, I could see when Dad and the doctor pulled in. Sitting against the strong bark of the tree, knees pulled to my chest, I waited. The house was quiet. The sun was now shining down on the rooftops. Dad had been gone for a while now. Tension was high; I could feel it.

Tilting my head, I could hear the sound of a car, or truck, coming in the distance. Standing, I waited to see if it was Dad. The church bells were ringing, almost drowning out the sound of the car. Suddenly, the soft humm of the motor turned into the most sickening sound. There was a long shrieking noise, followed by a hard thump and then screaming.

Jumping to my feet, I looked around wildly. 'Oh, Lord,' I thought in a panic, 'what has happened?'

My legs were weak as I tried to walk to the house. Momma threw the screen door open, almost tripping down the steps as she came to me.

"What was that, Annie?" Her voice trembled.

"I don't know, Momma," I answered her, now crying.

She took my hand, and Momma and I went around to the front of the store to look. Way up the road, where you started into town, we saw people gathered everywhere. We couldn't see what had been hit, but steam was rising in an angry swirl up into the air.

"Come on. I hope that's not your dad," she said, her voice breaking.

I really didn't want to see. My heart was pounding. Sweat was breaking out across my lips, and I felt like I was going be sick. But Momma pulled me along with her. Maybe she was scared too. When we were almost to the scene, Glen Ayers, the postmaster, saw us coming. Walking to us in quick pace, he stopped us before we got too close.

"Now, Lois, I'm gonna walk you and Annie back home. There's been an accident, and it's not something a little girl should see." Glen firmly took us by the arms and turned us around to go back the way we came. The mournful scream of a woman could be heard on that Sunday morning. "My baby, my baby!" Chills ran all over me.

"What happened, Glen?" By now, Momma was frantic.

"Lois, Cecil had an accident. Now, he's okay," he hurriedly added. "Just calm down. The sheriff will be bringing him home in a bit."

"Oh my God," Momma sobbed. "Ginny is having the baby. You sure he's okay?" She looked at Glen's face, fear jumping from her eyes.

"Yes, he has a bump on the head and a bloody nose, but Doctor Bailey is checking him out." He patted her on the back.

"Then, who's screaming, and why can't I go to him?" she questioned him.

"We'll talk about that later. Now, let's get y'all home and get y'all calmed down first." He smiled gently at me.

My body shook with sobs. My dad was hurt, my momma was crying, and Ginny was hurting badly. I caught a deep breath, but my body still shook.

We made it into the kitchen. Momma went to the sink, wetting her face with cool water, trying to calm down. I just crumbled at the table, laying my head down and taking deep breaths. Glen stood at the door as if he was on guard.

"I have to go check on Ginny." Momma tried to straighten her hair and smooth her dress. Leaning over, she put her arms around me. "It's okay, Annie. Everything's okay." Then, she hugged me and went down the hall to the stairs.

'It's Sunday. Nothing bad is supposed to happen on Sunday. Oh, how I wish we had never moved here,' I thought angrily. Glen started making coffee. Going to the electric stove, he turned it on. 'That's weird,' I thought to myself, 'I didn't know men made coffee or used a stove.' Turning and seeing the confused look on my face, he grinned.

"I live alone." He chuckled shyly. "I learned to use a stove and cook for myself a long time ago." He stared out the window, now lost in thought.

"When will they bring Dad, Mr. Glen?" He sat down in front of me at the table. Reaching across the table, he took my small hands into his large ones.

"It won't be long, sweetie, and don't you worry. Do you want me to get you anything? I can cook you up some eggs or something," he boasted, eyebrows raised.

"No, thank you." A smile broke out on my face in spite of my broken heart. I wanted to ask about the screaming woman, but I didn't. The sound was still fresh in my ears. I knew anything he said wouldn't be good. The smell of fresh brewed coffee filled the room, bringing a comforting feeling with it, like nothing had even happened. I heard the shuffling of feet overhead and looked up at the ceiling. Steps could be heard coming down the stairs. Nathan entered the kitchen, looking like a hemmed up, scared animal. He looked at Glen and tried to speak in a calm voice.

"Lois wants to know if you can boil some water. And, Annie, I need a clean white sheet and the sewing scissors."

Both of us quickly got up to get the things.

"Son, sit down here while we get this, and have some strong coffee." Glen guided Nathan to the table and then got started on the water. Next, he handed him a steaming cup of coffee. I rummaged around the sewing box until I found the scissors and then headed to the linen closet in the washroom for the clean sheet. When I came back into the kitchen, the water was already starting to boil on the stove, and Nathan was looking a little better, his hands hugging the cup of coffee.

"I'll help you carry it up, son," Glen offered.

Nodding, Nathan sat the cup down, and the two left the room. It wasn't long before Glen returned to his post in the kitchen.

"Listen, Annie. I'm going to fix up some eggs and toast. Little girls can't go without something in their bellies. You just sit right there and let me fix you a bite."

"Okay, Mr. Glen. I think I am getting a little hungry." My belly growled. Laughing, Glen went to the icebox and got the eggs, butter, and milk out to start cooking.

"Your folks ever let you have coffee?" he asked me sheepishly.

"No, I never ask for any." I looked at Glen, wondering what he meant.

"Well, I'm going to fix you a sip. Nothing makes things any calmer than a warm cup of coffee." He smiled. Shrugging my shoulders, I accepted his offer. I watched as he poured about half of a teacup for me. He stirred in a little milk and then added a couple teaspoons of sugar.

"See how you like that," he beamed, proud of himself. Slowly, I pursed my lips and took a sip. Glen waited, looking as if he was holding his breath. Licking my lips, I slowly smiled.

"Mr. Glen, that tasted just perfect. Everything is just right!" I was also shocked.

"No one has ever been able to refuse a cup of coffee from Glen Ayers," he answered in a confident voice as he cracked an egg in the pan. Laughing, I slowly enjoyed my first cup of coffee. At the first sizzle of the egg, Baby Andy made his first howl from upstairs. Even the air in the kitchen stood still for a second or two. Jumping up from the table, I ran for the stairs. Reaching the top, I could see that the bedroom door was closed. Creeping over, I held my ear to the door. I could hear all of them talking happily. I tapped on the door first, and then I opened it a crack. Ginny lay there, propped up on pillows like nothing had happened. Nathan stood at the window as the sun shined in on little Andy. He smiled down at him. Momma was gathering the evidence that a baby was born and tying it all up in a sheet.

"Come over here, Aunt Annie." Nathan smiled, looking like he had just won a teddy bear. Walking over, he sat on the edge of the bed to let me have a better view. Little wisps of golden-red hair lay all over his tiny head. His fist was settled in his mouth as he sucked hungrily. Leaning up, Ginny cooed to him.

"You want to hold him, Annie?" she asked.

"Yes!" I half squealed. Gently, I took him in my arms. My heart melted, and I fell in love instantly. Momma let me hold him for a minute, and then she said it was time for him to eat. After kissing him, I let Nathan take him and give him to Ginny.

Momma quietly shut the door. Smiling, Momma and I started down the stairs, heading to the kitchen. Glen was sitting at the table. Toast, eggs, and bacon were waiting on the table. Momma poured some coffee while I sat down to eat.

"Glen," she started in a serious voice, not even looking at him. "I'm going to wait a few more minutes, and if Cecil's not here, I'm going to him."

"Let me make a call," he said soothingly. "I'll see if they're on their way, okay?"

Nodding, she stood by the sink and looked out the window, sipping her coffee and looking like she had just about had enough. Glen spoke quickly into the phone, his voice low. Putting the receiver back, he turned to Momma.

"The doctor just gave him a shot, and Sheriff Bridges is bringing him on over."

"They'd better." Momma looked him straight in the eyes and didn't blink.

Silently, I nibbled at my food. Mr. Glen was a good cook.

CHAPTER 6

Dad came through the door, being led by Paul, a deputy of Sheriff Bridges. He looked horrible. A small cry left Momma's throat as she hurried to him. She touched his face all over, frantic and so confused. Questions tumbled out of her as she helped him to the sitting room to lie on the couch.

"You okay, honey?" she asked, about to cry.

"Yeah, I'm fine," he mumbled.

Momma could see he was in no shape to talk. He drifted off to sleep in seconds. She motioned to me and the deputy, and we went back to the kitchen.

"What in the world is wrong with him?" she hissed. I was so shocked and confused. I just stood far away from everyone.

Paul began what would be the most horrible story I had ever heard. My dad had been coming back from a farm to get the doctor. Doctor Bailey had told him to go ahead and that he would be right behind him. I guess Dad was trying to hurry and get back to help Momma. When he turned down the road coming into town, he started to slow down. At the same time, Chris, Ben Basker's little six-year-old son, was crossing the road, heading for the church. Dad's brakes failed. He couldn't stop. Out of fear, little Chris had stopped dead in the middle of the road. Dad swerved to miss him, but the back tire of the truck had struck Chris, going over his stomach. He died minutes later from internal bleeding.

Momma sat with her head down on the table and cried. I just stood and sobbed. 'So, that's what the screaming was about,' I thought, my mind whirling with images. 'My poor dad.' The deputy stood silently while the words broke our hearts. Finally, Glen came over and sat beside Momma.

"Lois..." He was fumbling for words. "It was an accident. Cecil did everything he could. The doctor gave him a shot for the shock. He was pretty torn up about it. You gotta be strong and help him through this, okay? He's going to need lots of love." Glen's voice was brittle. Momma could only nod. Her heart was broken for Dad, and it was Momma who was suffering now. I looked around and realized I hadn't even seen Nathan standing in the hallway. He had heard everything. Slowly, he walked into the kitchen, taking me into a hug as he patted my head gently. I cried more.

Soon, the men cleared out. Handing Momma a brown bottle of pills, Paul said to give Dad one if he got in bad shape. Momma looked at the bottle in a daze. Then, she just nodded her head. After they were gone, the three of us sat around the table. Nobody had anything to say for quite a while. Nathan had buttered a piece of the toast Glen had made and had started dipping it into his coffee as he ate it. When she noticed, Momma stood and looked at Nathan with embarrassment.

"Nathan, honey, I'm sorry. Let me fix you a bite to eat. You must be starved, and Ginny also has to eat for that baby." Her voice trembled. As she spoke, she was flying around the room, trying to gather some things to get started on the stove. Walking up behind her, Nathan turned her around and looked straight into her eyes.

"Lois, I'm fine. Now, you go sit with Cecil while I find something to make for Ginny. Annie will help me." Looking sideways, he winked at me and smiled. "Cecil needs you, and I know you want to keep an eye on him. Now, go ahead and go in there. And you're going to eat something too." Holding his hand up, he stopped her before she could speak. "You ain't gonna be no good for nobody if you don't keep your strength up," he persisted.

Momma didn't argue a bit. She fled the room to check on dad.

"Now, Annie, you and I are going to fix some soul food for these ladies," he said, winking again. "My momma made sure all my brothers and I could cook. Didn't want none of her babies starving, she said." He chuckled.

Nathan soon had me stirring, pouring, and turning food on the stove top. Before long, the knot in my stomach settled some. By now, it was well past noon, and the sky was looking like rain. 'Don't matter,' I thought. 'It's a terrible day anyways.' Soon, the sound of rain splattering on the roof could be heard. Every once in a while, Nathan took the dish towel that was slung across his shoulder and opened the oven door to check the biscuits. Taking the big fork, I removed the golden-brown bacon, placing it on a dish. Next, he poured a steaming hot pan of gravy into another bowl. He had heated up the leftover fried taters from the night before too. The kitchen smelled yummy. Even Momma stepped in the kitchen to look around. Seeing the table, her eyes opened wide.

"Lord, Nathan!" she exclaimed. "Who taught you to do all of this?" she asked, smiling.

"My momma." He laughed. "Now, I'm going take Ginny's food up. You and Annie can dig in, and then you can see if Cecil might eat a little." Nathan patted Momma's hand that was resting on the table, and then he started fixing Ginny's plate.

Momma and I sat down. Taking a biscuit, Momma poured a spoon of gravy, with bits of bacon in it, over the top. 'It's not the first time we've had breakfast for lunch,' I thought. Reaching for the big platter, I took a fried egg and a piece of crunchy bacon. I wanted to taste his gravy, so I put a small spoonful beside my egg. Looking at Momma, I noticed she wasn't being too picky about eating.

"Lord, Annie, I think he can cook as good as me!" She stopped eating to look at me and then went back to eating, picking up another piece of bacon. It made me feel even better to see her eating. Now, if we could get Dad to eat something, he might feel better too. Nathan came back down the stairs to join us.

"Watch out, girls. I'm as hungry as a hound pup," he said and began filling his plate up. "I see you find my cooking to your liking?" he questioned us with his eyebrows raised.

"It's delicious, Nathan," Momma gushed. He didn't answer. Instead, he just kept his fork working at a steady pace, bringing food from his plate to his mouth. After she finished, Momma got Dad a little gravy, a biscuit, and a hot cup of coffee.

"Want to come with me, Annie?" she asked.

"Tell you what...you ladies go on ahead. I'm going up to check on Ginny and the baby. Might take a nap." Nathan yawned.

"Go right ahead, Nathan. I'll wash up the dishes later; it will give me something to pass the time." Momma tried a weak smile. "Come on, Annie. Let's try to feed your dad a little."

Momma sat on the edge of the couch, placing the food on the little table beside her. I watched, hoping for the best. First, she spoke his name softly. His eyelashes fluttered some. Looking up at me, she smiled.

"Cecil," she cooed to him. "Wake up, honey. I need you to try and eat a bit for me." We waited. The knot on his head was now just the size of a small egg. His eye looked like it would turn black in a couple of days. "Cecil, wake up." She nudged his shoulder. Finally, his eyes slowly opened. Squinting, he tried to focus so he could see us better.

"Lois..." His voice was thin and crocky.

"It's okay, honey. You're here at home, resting nicely. I just wanted to see if you want to eat a bit," Momma explained.

Something wasn't right. His eyes were so blank, almost like the eyes of a blind person. He looked around like he was lost or something. Worried, I knelt down on my knees beside him, near Momma's feet.

"Hey, Dad..." I paused. "Take a sip of this good coffee. Glen says it makes everything better."

Momma raised his head a little and put the cup to his mouth. He sipped weakly.

"The baby..." Dad tried to raise himself up.

"Baby is fine, honey." Momma gently eased him back down. "You have a fine, healthy grandson, so you better get to eating some, okay?" She waited for a sign.

"Oh, Lois, honey." Tears eased down his eyes.

"Shhh, Cecil, we know all about it. You couldn't help it, honey. Was an accident." Momma tried to reassure him.

"Help me sit up a little, Lois."

Momma and I gently helped Dad sit up, putting a pillow behind his head. With both hands, he tried to rub the sleep from his face and eyes. Momma had a spoonful of bread and gravy waiting. Slowly, she put it to his mouth. Seeing her desperate look, he took it and began to chew as he looked into her eyes.

He didn't eat much, but it was a start. The food and coffee helped him become more alert and awake. Handing me the plate, Momma told me to start the dishwater, rake the scraps out, and then wait for her. Reaching up, Dad pulled me down to him, giving me a soft hug around the neck. My face beamed.

With a lighter heart, I began to clean up the table and stack the dishes up. Momma talked with Dad for a while, and then he lay back down, dozing back off to sleep. Momma told me to run upstairs and check on the baby while she washed and tidied up the kitchen. When I opened the door to their room, I saw that the three of them were relaxing on the bed, the baby in the middle and the mother and father on each side.

"How's Dad?" Ginny asked.

"Oh, I think he'll be okay. It might take some time, but he's a tough one," I answered. Sitting on the foot of the bed, I watched little Andy sleep. We talked about Dad, the accident, and little Chris. Nathan got up to take the chamberpot and empty it, letting me take his place beside Andy. Ginny and I talked about everything now that we were alone...the pain of having a baby, learning how to feed him, and then Dad again.

"You really think he's okay, Annie?" she whispered.

"No, and don't you repeat that either," I told her firmly. "His eyes look hollow and empty now, Ginny. Like he's there, but he's not."

"Nathan mentioned something like that, Annie—how some things can break a man...you know...in the head." Ginny looked scared as she spoke.

"We will just have to watch him, I guess," I answered. She nodded in agreement. Our hearts were heavy now. If it wasn't for Andy, we probably would have cried.

CHAPTER 7

The first two days were slow. With Nathan's help, Momma got Dad upstairs to bed that first night. After a good night of rest, he looked a little better. Still, he sometimes looked like he was miles away. We all tried to take his mind off of it. Some days, little Andy was the only thing that made him smile. Nathan was running the store. Since his family ran their own business, it came natural to him. I just thought Nathan had a nack for running things. Sometimes, Dad would go into the store and sweep or dust things off, but when business got busy, he would slip back into the house. It seemed like he thought people of the town blamed him, and he was worried about confronting them.

September was here, and soon, school would start. I really didn't care now. I just wanted to go home...back to where things had been calm, where we had a routine and life was so simple. My grandmother once said, "Be careful what you wish for," and, boy, she was right. Forget all the pretty dresses, the big school, and all the candy and things. I would trade it all for home. Momma found me sitting on the back steps, deep in thought. Sitting down beside me, she put her arm around me and pulled me close.

"What's wrong, Annie?" she gently asked.

"I just want to go home," I said, now sobbing.

"Shhh, now, I know how you feel. I'll let you in on a little secret since you feel the same as me and your dad," she whispered.

"You guys want to go too?" I whispered back.

"Well, we've been thinking. Nathan does a good job running the store. Maybe we could let him and Ginny live here and run the place, and we could move back. Of course, we would divide the earnings from the store with them. And they could visit us any time and bring little Andy."

"Oh my gosh, Momma. That would be so great!"

"Shhh...be quiet now." She smiled. "We didn't know you would be excited about it," she said.

I wrapped my arm around my momma's tiny frame and hugged her tightly.

"I'll talk to your dad tonight and let him know you want to go too. He will be so relieved." Tears filled her eyes. She patted my head and stood to go back into the house. "Why don't you go play with Timmy?" She held the screen door open, waiting for my answer.

"I think I will." I smiled, feeling like a load had been lifted off of me.

Jumping off the porch, I skipped around the side of the store and then off through the field that led to Timmy's house. They lived on a dirt road leaving town, out next to some farms. I hadn't bothered to put shoes on. I just wanted to be the old me. Free and happy. Walking along the road, I gazed at the pretty daisies and wildflowers growing in the now browning, tall grass. Lost in the joy I felt, I didn't hear the truck until it was right behind me. Slowing, the man chugged the truck to a stop. Leaning out the window, Ben Bakster's face was looking straight into mine. My heart fluttered, not knowing what to expect. We hadn't seen him since the accident, when his son, Chris, had been killed.

"Hey there...going somewhere?" He grinned, a friendly look on his face.

"Just to my friend Timmy's. It's up the road a piece," I answered cautiously.

"Well, hop in. I'll drop you off. Going that way myself!" He didn't seem to know who I was. "Come on. You'll get there quicker." He grinned and winked. I looked around and started walking to the other side of the truck. Opening the door, I hopped in. The least I could do was be nice. Putting the truck in gear, he eased to a slow crawl, heading down the road.

"Summer's about over. Won't be long till school starts," he continued as I sat still and watched him. "Are you excited?" he asked.

"Oh, a little, I guess." My voice seemed to echo in the cab of the truck.

"Chris used to get so excited. Course, he had only gotten to go one term." His face had lost the jolly expression. Getting a little nervous, I didn't know how to answer him. I sure didn't want him to find out who I was, so I pretended not to know.

"Maybe he will be just as excited this year," I answered, not knowing my words would ignite a fury in him.

"You think I don't know who you are?" he sneered. Scared, I backed away and pushed myself closer to the door. I could feel the window crank grinding into my hip.

"Sir, I think I should get out here." My voice broke as I reached for the door handle.

"No, no, you ain't getting out here." He shifted into a higher gear, and the truck sped up, bouncing me around in the seat as it went over the bumpy dirt road. "Your daddy's gonna pay for what he did, even if he has to pay with his own blood!" he shouted. I was crying hard now.

"Please!" I pleaded. "It was an accident. My daddy wouldn't hurt no one!"

"Shut up! You hear me? Shut up!" Tears were coming down his cheeks, just like the tears coming down mine.

He turned down a little road on the left, and we disappeared into the shade of the trees. He was nervous, jerking and grinding the gears as he neared an old barn sitting in the corner of a small, cleared piece of ground. He came to a hard stop, and I was thrown forward, busting my mouth on the dashboard. The taste of blood seeped into my mouth, mixing with the salty tears. I felt dizzy with fear. Grabbing a piece of hay string, he grabbed my hands and quickly tied them together. My mouth was mumbling, "Momma. Oh, Momma." My chin fell to my chest. Ben sat there, one hand on the steering wheel, the other shaking as he rubbed his stubbly face over and over. His body shook with the grief inside him. Trying to compose himself, he angrily opened the truck door and then came around to my side. I couldn't move; I couldn't look at his face. He scooped me up, and I hid my face close to my armpit. I didn't want to see what was coming or where we were going. I just cried for Momma.

When we entered the barn, I heard the squeaky sound of a door opening, and I could smell the old hay, mixed with the familiar scent of livestock that had once been here. Bending low, he entered a small stall and sat me down. With my head still down, I could see the dusty dirt drifting in the shards of sunlight coming through the weathered boards of the barn. Slowly raising my head, I saw him squatting on his heels, not looking at me. Instead, he looked straight ahead like he didn't know what to do. He angrily ducked back out of the door, and quickly, before he changed his mind, he shut the door tightly.

I started crying again, realizing he was going to leave me here. "Please let me out, Mr. Ben," I begged. Then, I heard the lock click. His footsteps hurried away from the barn. Weak and shaking, I scooted to the corner, leaning my head over and resting it on the warm wood. I didn't feel like I could even hold it up myself. Hands still tied, I wiped my face and mouth with the back of my hands. My upper lip felt a little swollen, but it wasn't bleeding now. Looking around, I could see I was in a small stall that was usually kept for a calf. 'Surely, Dad will find me,' I thought. But I knew that they would be thinking I was at Timmy's...playing and having fun. No one would even think this was happening. I would have never thought this could happen either. I just leaned there. Would he come back? Would he be angrier when he did? Now, I was getting scared again. 'Stay calm...just stay calm,' I told myself. 'If I'm really quiet, he might not bother me if he comes back.' Soon, my eyes became heavy, weak from the shock of what felt like a nightmare. I thought about Andy. Taking a deep breath, I thought of his rosy cheeks, soft skin, and rings of red curls. Soon, I fell asleep, exhausted.

"Annie...Annie." In my sleep, the voice sounded very far away. "Annie!" I jumped awake. Looking around wildly, I searched for the sound again, turning my head every which way. *Tap tap tap.* A low sound came from the outside wall.

"Who's there?" I hissed, trying to be quiet.

"It's Timmy. You okay, Annie?"

"Oh my Lord, Timmy!" I began to cry. "Timmy, he locked me in. Ben locked me in!"

"I know. I was watching. I was headed to your house when I saw you, and then the truck stopped. So, I watched and then followed him. I had to make sure he was gone before I could come to you. From what I could see, he's watching your place from the diner. I didn't get too close!" he whispered loudly.

"Oh God, get me out, Timmy. Please!" And I cried harder.

"Calm down. I brought a hammer. I'm going to try and loosen a couple of boards so you can crawl out, okay?"

Scanning the boards, I saw Timmy's eyes straining to look through the crack in the boards. Only slits of his eyes could be seen, but they were the most beautiful things I had seen that day. My heart pounded with excitement now.

"My hands are tied," I explained.

"We'll worry about that later." he assured me.

Timmy worked and pried on the rusty nails as fast as his young hands could go. They squeaked and groaned as he pulled with the hammer. At last, one board fell sideways, still held by one nail. I shoved my hands through.

"Hurry and untie me first. I can't stand it!" My hands shook until Timmy grabbed them and held them still. Taking his pocket knife, he cut the string loose. It fell to the ground, leaving my hands feeling weightless. Shoving my hair from my face, I waited while he worked on the next board. If a branch groaned, he stopped, not even breathing until it felt safe. Finally, the next board fell loose. My blood rushed through my body with relief. And there was Timmy, sweat beading on his face while he fought the tears in his eyes. He helped me out, and we maneuvered my skinny frame through the opening. Taking my hand, Timmy began running, practically dragging me along. The brush and rocks tore at my feet, but I didn't care. I was free. I was going home.

CHAPTER 8

Timmy stopped behind a large tree, pulling me close to him. After peeping around both sides, he relaxed and tugged a small canteen from his back pocket before handing it to me.

"Drink some, Annie," he urged. Throwing my arms around his neck, I hugged him tight, tears falling again.

"You're okay now," he soothed, drying my eyes with his thumbs. The cool water felt good on my dry throat. "Did that dog bust your lip, Annie?" Timmy asked, looking mad now.

"No..." I paused, breathing slow to calm myself. "The truck stopped quickly and threw me into the dash. Are we going to my house now?" I asked him.

"No, we got to stay low for a bit. He's watching. We'll sneak around and see what's going on first. We have to be careful, Annie. He's not in his right mind right now, okay?" He took my hand, giving me a small grin. "I'm not going to let nothing happen to you. Come on."

"Look, Annie, right between the post office and bank." He waited while I followed his pointing finger. Sure enough, there he was, leaned back on the bench, as if waiting for the sun to go down. Chills ran all over me.

"Let's see if we can make it to the back of your house, okay?" Nodding, I followed him. Like shadows, we crept along the tree line to the back of the house. Except for Timmy's eyes looking through those boards, nothing had ever looked better than the sight of my home.

"Now, when I say go, we will both run for the house." He spoke low now, his hand tightening on mine. Once more, I nodded to him. I waited.

"Go!" The words came low but loud. When Timmy jerked the screen door open, he literally pulled it loose from the hinges. Momma had a bowl of sliced taters in her hand and was headed for the stove, and the pieces shattered as it hit the floor. I ran to her and heard Timmy lock the door behind us. Bewildered, she picked me up when I reached her, locking her arms around me.

"What's going on?" she demanded from Timmy as I lay on her shoulder and cried.

"Oh, Momma. Momma," I cried.

"Cecil!" she hollered. Dad came running from the hall. Timmy had slid to the floor and had started crying too. He had held up as long as he could.

"She okay?" Dad hurriedly asked Momma.

"I don't know. They just came tearing through the door!" she shrieked. Momma stepped around the mess to where Dad had squatted down next to Timmy.

"Annie, honey, calm down. It's okay now. What happened? Did a bear chase you, or did a snake get after you?" she asked. I couldn't answer. I just shook my head back and forth, telling her no. Finally, Timmy caught his breath. "It was worse than that." He was sobbing now. Sitting down on the floor beside him, Dad hugged him gently. "Tell us what happened, son," he said softly.

Slowly, Timmy got the story out. Dad was standing now, cussing and threatening to go kill Ben, when a rapid knocking came from the door. Dad pulled it open, pushing Timmy away from the door. There stood Polly, Timmy's mom, wringing her hands and looking around wildly.

"Oh my Lord, are they okay?" Her words trembled. Kneeling down, she caressed Timmy's face and hugged him. Momma had sat down in a kitchen chair, still holding me, now crying with me.

"The sheriff found Ben sitting on that cock-eyed bench in front of the diner, crying and going on about what he had done. Mr. Brown came out and said he saw them run in here, so I ran over. That man just lost it, Lois. He doesn't even know everything he's done. Dr. Bailey is having somebody take him on over to the hospital in Wilkes county. He will be over here in a minute to check on the kids." Polly was out of breath from talking so fast. Dad just shook his head.

Momma and Polly washed our faces and gave us glasses of cold milk for our stomachs. Momma checked my busted lip and said it wasn't too bad but that it would be sore. Dad had rolled a smoke and stood, looking out of the back door and waiting. The screen door lay crookedly against the side of the house. Soon, Sheriff Bridges and Dr. Bailey pulled in. Dad waited and then stepped aside as they entered the kitchen.

"Come here. Let me check you babies out." Dr. Bailey beckoned to me and Timmy with his hand. He asked us a few questions, listened to our hearts, and looked us over. "I think all you two need is some rest. Maybe a nice hot bath and warm milk." He smiled. Everybody smiled. The sheriff said Ben was gone. They would take charge when he got back...if he did. After some coffee, they left. Polly took Timmy home after Dad gave him a sack of candy for his heroism in rescuing me. We hugged each other with a promise to see each other soon.

"Where are Ginny and Nathan?" I asked, looking towards the hall.

"They went home to show off the baby and get some more things," Momma answered.

"Annie, we're going home tomorrow. I've had enough of town life." Dad spoke like he was exhausted.

"Me too, Dad. I'd go tonight if I could."

"Well, let's get started packing then." Momma jumped up excitedly. "I can't wait either."

They both hugged and kissed me, thanking the Lord I was okay. Then, we went to gather our things.

Dad had already made a deal with Nathan on a car, and they were driving it back the next day when they came home. Dad didn't want anything to do with a truck, so Nathan offered to haul our big stuff back later. I slept right in the middle of Momma and Dad that night. They just wanted me close. I tossed and turned a little and then fell asleep knowing that soon I would be back on the mountain where home really was.

About the Author

Elizabeth Hardin Buttke holds a diploma in Medical Records and was also a substitute teacher. She is the author of *Deep in the Holler*. *Tell Me a Story* is her second book of short stories from her childhood. She is currently working on short stories and a novel. You may contact her through Facebook under *Elizabeth Hardin Buttke*, or email at: ebuttke@yahoo.com.